SALLY GARDNER

MY SIDE of the DIAMOND

HOT KEY BOOKS

First published in the UK in 2017
This paperback edition published 2018 by
HOT KEY BOOKS
80–81 Wimpole Street
London W1G 9RE

Text © Sally Gardner, 2017
Illustrations © Nat Barlex, 2017

A CIP catalogue record for this book is available from the British Library.

ISBN: 978-1-4714-0681-2
also available as an ebook

1

Designed by Perfect Bound Ltd
Printed and bound in Great Britain by Clays Ltd, Elcograf S.p.A.

Hot Key Books is an imprint of Bonnier Zaffre Ltd,
a Bonnier Publishing company
www.bonnierpublishing.com

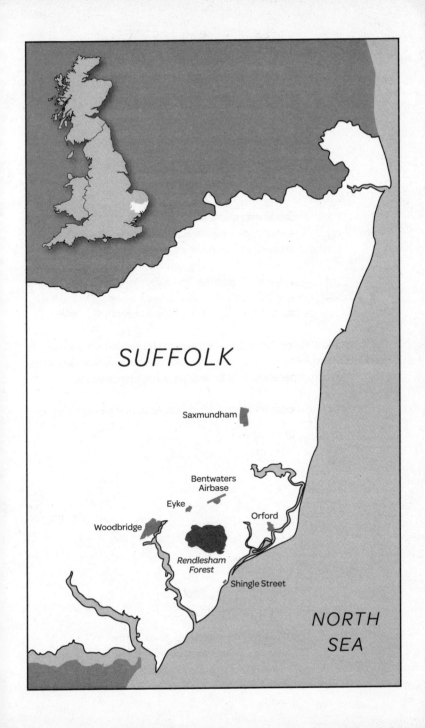

To Freya with all my love, SG

JAZMIN LITTLE

Chapter One

Judge me, hate me, find me unforgiven. You won't be the first. I have lived with it long enough. It changes nothing. Becky Burns was my best friend. My soul sister, my blood. I knew her better than anyone else – or I thought I did.

She didn't like heights. I heard once that if you dropped a stone off the Eiffel Tower, it hit the pavement at the speed of a bullet. Lord knows what the effect of two people jumping from that height would be. Most probably like a bomb going off – if they landed, that is.

I dream of Becky a lot. I'm still angry with her, angry with Icarus, angry with myself. Angry with all those who disregarded my story and accused me of being an unreliable witness.

I'm only human – fallible, full of mistakes.

Ruth wished the past to be washed away, wanted to bleach out my presence, my narrative. I have the right to my story. It was mine and Becky's, not Ruth's. She wasn't even there.

At the inquest I was left voiceless, my evidence mocked. In the end I kept schtum, especially when those lawyers went at me. I only said what they wanted to hear and no more. Still they ate me up and spewed me out. There were calls for me to be sent to trial. Ruth would have loved to see me burn at the stake. She'd have been the first with a box of matches.

Which paper did you say you were from, Mr . . . er . . . Jones?

Oh, what kind of research? Is it for a UFO organisation?

It was so long ago, surely everything there is to say about it has been said or written.

Who else are you interviewing?

You know, I'm not the only one on your list who was laughed out of court. I see you're going to talk to Mari Scott. She knew Skye and Lazarus quite well. At the inquest the lawyer accused her of speaking ill of the dead, dismantling their good characters. I learned the hard way, that's what lawyers do – specialise in making you look stupid, cruel, careless.

The law is such a cold language. Who are they to judge others? Above and below my mistakes, I thought then that I did the right thing. Now I'm not so sure. Time has dragged up more questions than answers.

When it happened, this man from the *Daily Mail* sat outside our block of flats and followed me everywhere. He offered me money. I didn't tell Mum. I know what she would have said: take it, we need it. But I couldn't. I told him to get lost.

No, I never spoke about her, not to any of the newspapers, or any of the others that came afterwards. As I said, Becky Burns was my best friend.

Chapter Two

I met her at school when we were eleven. Her parents were socialists; they agreed with comprehensive education. They could afford to because they got tutors for anything that was lacking. Not that Becky needed tutoring. They lived in this really smart house in Camden Town, all scrubbed floors and Farrow & Ball colours. You know, like Elephant's Breath. Bloody stupid name. We just had mould in our flat. Now, that looked to me like Elephant's Breath – all black and blotchy.

I didn't take much notice of Becky Burns when we started at Morsefield Secondary School. We were both in Mr Hallow's class. She was thin, with dark, bobbed hair that hung down in sheets either side of her face. She never much pulled back the blinds to look out. We called her Moleskine. She didn't have any friends. There were roughly three gangs in our year: the nerds who were going to do very well and go to university; my gang, who were going particularly nowhere, and then there were the arty ones. We left them alone. But Becky didn't fall into any of those gangs. She sat outside them all, writing in her Moleskine book. Come on, who at eleven writes in a Moleskine book?

Anyway, she wrote in it all the time. Her mum would come and pick her up in a four-by-four. My mum never could be bothered to pick me up, ever.

Comprehensive, yeah. You get to see how the other half live, that's for shizzle.

Becky Burns irritated me rotten then, she and that little black book of hers. She wrote on those small squares in tiny letters, a traffic jam of words. One day in the playground, I found her sitting on a step, minding her own business, probably hoping I wouldn't see her. I went up to her and took her Moleskine book away.

'What are you going to do about it?' I said.

She said nothing, not a word, not even 'Give it back.'

She just stood up and went into the class. I thought she was about to report me to Mr Hallow but she didn't. I took the notebook home.

There was a row going on in my flat that evening. My older sister, Kylie, lived with us, with her baby, Sam. She was separated from his dad, who was only eighteen when he became a father. Kylie had been sixteen. He and his mates came round every now and again, shouted abuse at our window, threw stones, that kind of juvenile thing. Once Mum had to call the police.

I went to my room and had a tin of cold baked beans for dinner. I quite like baked beans, prefer them cold. Hate hot baked beans. I sat in the bedroom that I shared with Sam and started to read what Becky had written. I was blown away – I mean, it was really awesome. I just wanted more. Next day I handed the Moleskine notebook back to her.

She looked up at me through the curtain of hair and said, 'Thank you.'

Nothing more. After that, I think I rather fixated on her. I talked to her about her story. It was about a different world, with these strange creatures that were like us, but weren't us. They came from outer space. I said I thought it was fantastic. She said it had all been done before, she'd just nicked everything from the sci-fi stories she'd read and collaged bits together with superglue – all the crazy things that interested her. She said it was something to do in a plastic world.

I thought that was kind of weak or really smart, and as I wasn't sure which, I said, 'Yeah, you're right.'

Becky gave me another of her Moleskines to read. I was really gripped.

I said, 'This is sick, better than *Doctor Who*, and really scary.'

Then she said, 'Would you like to come back for tea?'

I'll never forget her mum picking us up in that four-by-four.

The Burnses' house was well old, a Victorian thing with very tall windows. Such a beautiful house. They even had a housekeeper to keep it beautiful. Becky's mum, Ruth – that's what Becky called her, that's what I called her: Ruth – she worked on a magazine, I think it was *Vogue*. Becky's dad, Simon, was an architect. They talked about politics and art, and they didn't argue, and they didn't have Heinz baked beans for tea, cold or hot.

Well. Fast forward.

I got thrown out by my mum when I was about fifteen. I didn't know what to do. Didn't want to sleep rough. Kylie and Sam had left by then. I think Mum just wanted some space before she went stir crazy. It was a small flat. I asked a few of my mates if I could stay the night but it became awkward. Their parents would say, 'Hasn't she got a home to go to?'

I never asked Becky though. I told her what had happened but I never asked.

Then she said, 'Why don't you come and live with me?'

I was really nervous, thought her mum and dad would kick up a fuss. Turns out it went with their socialist principles that I should live with them. They gave me my own room. Like, why? My own room – I'd never had that, ever. Becky gave me some of her clothes to wear. We had wicked fun together, and we talked about her story a lot.

And just for a laugh, I said, 'Why don't you put it up on Facebook?' She wasn't keen, but I said, 'You've nothing to lose.'

So we did. The next day, after school, we discovered it had two thousand likes. I mean, that's stupid.

There were lots of comments too – like, 'We want more.'

Becky said, 'I don't want to do it again.' I asked her why not, and she shrugged. 'Not ready,' she said.

I feel bad about this part. I never really told anyone this but it's bugged me rotten. Becky's mum, Ruth, was one of the people who read it online.

She said, 'Becky, everyone is waiting for the next chapter.'

Becky said, 'That's so stupid, it's pathetic. It doesn't mean anything.'

Ruth was so nice to me for the whole week, asking if I was all right, if I needed pocket money, and on it went.

At the end of the week, she said, 'Jazmin, would you do something for me? Would you tell me where Becky keeps her Moleskine notebooks?'

And I did. Becky told me later that the next thing she knew all six chapters had been put on Whatwrite. You know, that website where you put up stories, poems, that kind of thing. People vote for the ones they would like to read more of. Yeah, you guessed it: Becky's story won outright.

By then it was the summer holidays. I've an aunt, Auntie Karen, who lives in Margate – she looked after Kylie and me when she could. She invited me down. Becky came to the seaside with me for a while. She liked my aunt. She told me I was lucky that I didn't have pushy parents. Then she had to go on holiday with her family. They were going to New York and then off to some swanky island that you can only get to in a little plane.

I stayed on with my Auntie Karen. I had nowhere else to go. Finally she called my mum down to Margate after Becky left. She said I was too young to be homeless and that my mum had responsibilities. They had a right bargy. You see, Auntie Karen never had children but she wanted them. Mum never wanted children but she had them. She said it was bad luck; I would say it was more to do with forgetting birth control. Auntie Karen told my mum what was what and Mum looked a bit sheepish. I think my aunt gave her some money so she could manage. Anyway, I went home with Mum to London and the flat.

All that summer, I never heard from Becky. Not a postcard, nothing. I was certain Ruth must have told her it was me who as good as handed over the Moleskines, though she'd promised it would be our secret.

I checked it online – I couldn't believe the number of views those chapters had had. One million – that was phenomenal. I tried to contact Becky through Facebook because she never answered texts. Still nothing.

When school started in the autumn, Becky wasn't there. The first day, some people said she'd left and gone to a private school. I knew her parents wouldn't do that. They were strong on state education, even if they did drink champagne. Ruth said all people are the same, or something like that. But Becky Burns definitely wasn't the same when she came back to school three weeks late. She wouldn't tell me where she'd been. I asked her again and again and all she said was that she wished everything could be like it was before.

'Before what?' I asked.

She said it didn't matter. I thought maybe she didn't like me any more, maybe she'd gone off me. I just couldn't work out what was wrong. It made me feel like I was nothing.

No teacher made an example of her for being absent. Maria McCoy had nearly been expelled for starting back at school late without a proper sick note.

Becky was distant. She didn't eat, just played with her food. I was worried about her. She wasn't like me – I blurt everything out, can't keep it in. It was nearly half-term before she invited me for tea at her house. I was so relieved. Pathetic, I know.

We were listening to 'Walk on the Wild Side'. She liked that song.

I said, 'Why aren't you writing in your Moleskine notebooks?'

'That was then,' she said. 'This is now.'

I asked her if we were still friends.

She said, 'Of course. You're my best friend – my only friend – in all the world.'

Still she never told me. I only found out at the end of the autumn term. It was all in the papers. Even the head of our school said he felt very proud that there was such a fine young writer among us.

The only person who didn't seem to be too thrilled was Becky. Her book, *The Martian Winter*, was to be published in February. There was already a film deal.

'Why didn't you say?' I said. 'That's fantastic.'

'Because I knew you would say that. And you would've agreed with Ruth that I shouldn't waste such an opportunity, and all that shit.'

That was the only thing she ever said about it. I think she knew what I'd done. In a way, I'm part of the reason Becky Burns jumped.

Chapter Three

The Martian Winter became a bestseller. At first it was a bit of a laugh, sort of unbelievable. Becky went from having one best friend – me – to her entire class claiming that each one of them knew her better than anyone else. That's what fame does – everyone wants a slice of that cake. The press sat outside the school gates with long-lens cameras. It was too much in every way. Way too much.

The book went to the top of the charts here and in America – it sold five million copies. Becky said, if books were bricks, how many cheap, unsound houses could she have built by now? I hadn't a clue. She said that it was a theoretical question.

Becky became thinner and more locked inside herself. She hated all the fuss. Because she was a minor, Crossbow Books, her publishers, appointed this young woman called Laura to assist her and she spent her time making sure that Becky was 'in the zone', as she called it. She meant interviews and that kind of stuff. But no matter what the interviewers asked her, Becky stayed schtum. You have to talk in interviews; silence isn't what anyone wants to hear. So they stopped trying to interview her. I suppose that just added to her mystery. It certainly didn't stop people writing a load of crap, all that psychobabble about the tortured young writer. What was wrong with everyone? She hadn't even taken her GCSEs.

I sort of lost touch with her. She wasn't at school that much and then she left. Ruth had her tutored at home. I suppose it was to appease her guilt about betraying her socialist principles that she wrote an article in the *Guardian* about her genius daughter being bullied. Like, yeah, a brain-breaking stupid thing to do, if you ask me.

I did my GCSEs and was trying to get a part-time job while waiting for my results when Becky texted me, asking if I'd like to spend the summer with her in somewhere called Orford. She added, 'Please say yes, otherwise Mum will insist on coming with me.'

I knew it must be bad – she never called Ruth 'Mum'.

I texted her back, saying I had to find work.

She said, 'Ruth will pay better than any summer job.' That was weird and I said I didn't need paying to come and see her.

'Just come then,' she texted back. 'I baked you a cake.'

I didn't know where Orford was and had to look it up. You know England's got this huge, round bottom that sticks out into the North Sea? That's Suffolk, an open invitation to a UFO. It couldn't miss a bum as big as that.

I was picked up that evening and driven there in the four-by-four. Not by Ruth but by a driver called Alan who now worked for the Burnses full time. They could afford that and more.

I hadn't seen Becky in a while and I was shocked. She was

stick-bone thin. It put you off eating to look at her. The cake was waiting for me. It had a small cement mixer's load of icing on top.

'It's only for you,' said Becky.

I knew she wasn't well, it was obvious. She sat at the end of the scrubbed wooden table in the huge kitchen and watched me eat the cake.

'What does it taste like?' she asked, staring at the cake.

'Crap,' I said. 'It tastes like crap. And I'm not playing this game.'

'What game?' she said.

'The game where I eat for you. If you want to know what the cake tastes like, you eat it.'

I pushed the plate towards her.

She laughed. 'You haven't changed.'

'No,' I said. 'Unlike you.'

I stormed out of the kitchen through the French windows, past the spot where the lights come on automatically, into the darkness. Bloody hell, it was proper night out there. No hum, no orange glow, just a sky with a sneeze-full of stars. I had taken three packets of my mum's fags, the ones she bought when she went to Gibraltar. I struck a match. Even a flicker of light was comforting in that abyss.

Becky came out and stood beside me with a torch in one hand and a plate with a slice of cake on it in the other.

'It makes you feel so small when you look up,' she said. 'Small and amounting to nothing.'

'I'm not your nanny,' I said. 'If you don't eat, you'll be ill, and

19

I'm not spending my summer messing about with all that.'

'All what?' said Becky, wide-eyed and far from innocent.

'My sister Kylie had bulimia and that was bad enough. I don't want the job of nurse. So I'm going home tomorrow.'

Becky picked up the slice of cake and took a bite.

'Too sweet,' she said.

'Yeah. As I said, it tastes like crap.'

We both started to laugh. We found a bottle of wine – yes, you guessed it, the Burnses had a wine cellar. The combination lock was dead simple to crack: Becky's birthday. Did her parents really think we were that stupid? We got drunk and I made popcorn. We sat outside. It was a warm night and Becky told me she did want to be a writer, just not now, but after she'd lived a bit. Ruth expected her to go to Oxford but Becky wanted to go to the University of East Anglia like her half-brother.

Wait. Rewind. I should have mentioned Alex. It's just that he wasn't around much when I lived at the Burnses' house. Becky's dad was his father. Ruth and Mari, Alex's mum, had been best friends back in the days when they were at art school. How Ruth qualified as a best friend I'm not sure. She nicked Mari's husband so I would call that a prize enemy. Alex was two and a half years older than Becky. He stayed away from Ruth and his dad as much as possible. You couldn't blame him. Ruth would always introduce him as her stepson. You'd think 'stepson' was his name, it was used that often. I'd met Alex for the first time around the Christmas before Becky's book was published. He and Ruth were like two cats in an alley full of fish arguing over one salmon. Becky.

I remember him shouting, 'You will send her over the edge if you don't stop pushing.'

I was a bit scared of Alex. He was dead fit, he said what he thought and he didn't care about the consequences.

At supper one evening, Ruth and Simon were talking about politics. I zoned out when those two started up. Not Alex. He pounced on them.

'Your crappy 1970s socialism. I hate any "ism" that's related to religion, and politics is a cancer as far as I am concerned, an evil that's infecting this world. We will be nullified by dullerism if we're not careful.'

Ruth told him to go to his room. He laughed, left the table and caught a train home. I didn't see him again until that summer I was in Orford.

Fast forward. As I said, we found a bottle of wine and I listened to all Becky had to say. We fell asleep on the sofa and were woken the next morning by Becky's mobile. Then mine rang. We ignored them. Then the house phone rang and finally Becky answered it. It was Ruth calling to remind us that Mark, the chimney sweep, was due at ten. Were we up, had Becky eaten, was she all right, had Jazmin arrived? I heard all this because Becky put her on speaker.

We were having breakfast and being a bit silly when the doorbell rang. I had boiled eggs and I'd cut the toast into soldiers. I was doing aeroplane noises, flying the soldiers at Becky to make her eat the egg. We'd forgotten all about the chimney sweep until I opened the door. If it hadn't been for the bag of brushes and the toolbox he carried, I'd have thought he was a salesman. He wasn't young. He had short grey hair and glasses. A neat freak, didn't look like a sweep, but I suppose I had this Victorian image of a man covered in soot. He was an advert for washing powder.

Becky was pleased to have an excuse not to eat her egg and toast.

'I mean it,' I whispered. 'You'll be all on your ownsome if you don't eat.'

She took the toast to the sofa and nibbled it. She asked Mark if he'd always been a chimney sweep. He said it was a new venture for him. He said it was good to be out and meeting people.

'What did you do before?'

He seemed reluctant to answer and told us he was known for being one of the cleanest chimney sweeps in the Woodbridge area.

Becky pulled her knees up and asked him again, but he still he didn't say much.

I offered him coffee and while I was in the kitchen I could hear Becky asking question after question. He was old school. I could tell that he didn't like talking about himself. At last, Mark said he'd worked for the prison service.

Now, if it had been me, I would have left it at that, but not Becky. She wanted to know more, and being smart, she knew how to get the answers. She reminded me of a tin-opener. With each question she cut a bit more round his lid until all the beans spilled out.

He told her he'd been looking after a prisoner who'd been in solitary confinement for years. I thought, what a boring job.

Recently this prisoner had been moved into an open prison nearby. Becky asked what he'd done.

Mark hesitated for a long time and then said, 'Do you remember the story of the two teenagers from round here – Skye and Lazarus?'

OK – that interested me. I mean, who hadn't heard of those two? The lovebirds who jumped or fell or were pushed off the dome of St Paul's Cathedral. If you put it in Google, hundreds of sites pop up. Some say that they never jumped, others that they're being held prisoner somewhere far away. Then there are those who are certain that they were taken by a UFO. Yeah, a lot of hocus-pocus.

Becky pretended to look as gormless as a crab in a bucket.

I said, 'You mean those two kids who jumped off St Paul's?'

'They didn't jump,' said Mark, unpacking his brush and rods. 'They were pushed.'

'But they never landed,' said Becky.

'They must have landed,' I said. 'If they were pushed off St Paul's, they'd have landed.'

Mark said nothing.

Becky had that Moleskine look on her, the one she had when she was writing.

'What's the name of the prisoner?' she asked.

Mark said, 'Go outside and see if the brush pops out the top of the chimney. That'll show there's no obstruction.'

We trooped out in our jim-jams and slippers. Sure enough, chim-chiminey and all that, there it was. Mary Poppins, eat your heart out.

We went back inside. Mark was putting away his kit.

'The prisoner, the man who pushed them off the roof – what was he called?' Becky asked.

I knew the answer. I mean, you'd have to have lived in a bubble not to know it.

His name was Icarus.

Chapter Four

It rained a lot in Orford. That's English summers for you. Becky lit fires and sat, writing in her Moleskine, not eating, not speaking.

I found Simon's computer in his study. The password was the same as the wine cellar's. Pathetic. After looking at sites with all the clothes that I couldn't afford, I checked the gossip columns. And then I put into Google 'Icarus Old Bailey'. Do people really have nothing better to do with their time? There were conspiracy theories and non-conspiracy theories and they all centred on what happened when Lazarus and Skye were pushed off the dome of St Paul's Cathedral. They'd never been to London before, having lived all their lives around Woodbridge, and the first thing they did, according to the *Daily Mail*, was get a taxi to St Paul's, where Icarus was waiting for them. When I thought about it, it gave me the creeps because it made no sense. Look, call me old fashioned but if you were sixteen and you found yourself in London for the first time, no way would you want to see some old cathedral. And if you were going to jump from a high building into oblivion, wouldn't you choose one where you had less chance of getting caught? It was the day before the Lord Mayor's Show, there were cameras everywhere, set up to record the parade. The video shot that day is still on YouTube. You can see Lazarus and Skye standing on the edge of the dome, holding hands, and behind them is a man later identified as Icarus. In the clip it shows him quite clearly pushing Skye and Lazarus off the dome. OK so far – two and two are making four and not yet adding up to weird. Still hand-in-hand, Skye and Lazarus begin to fall. Someone had the bright idea of freeze-framing the shot. It shows them suspended in the air, then what appears to be a flash of light – then nothing. Now, if you believe that two and two make four you have to accept that if two people jump from the dome of St Paul's, they would be bound to land. They'd be dead but they would land. This is where it gets really freaky and the physics doesn't work. Two people jumped from the dome of St Paul's, witnessed by many. No one lands. Icarus was arrested and charged with murder, though what happened to Skye and Lazarus was never properly explained. The conspiracy theorists went into meltdown.

So here we go, the top-ten loony tunes of what happened to those two flightless love birds:

One: they were kidnapped by aliens.

Two: it was a magic trick and they're both alive and well.

Three: they're being held in a secret prison.

Four: they were a couple of holograms and an innocent man was sent to prison.

Five: they were angels.

Six: it was a forewarning of the end of the world.

Seven: it was a cover-up by MI5 and the CIA.

Eight: it's all to do with the Bermuda Triangle.

Nine: they were fairies and fairies are really aliens.

Ten: the answer lies in the writings of Icarus, which so far have proved impossible to decode.

A load of rubbish, that's what I thought back then in the rain-soaked days in Orford. The day I lost my rag with Becky was the day the sun came out for a minute.

Becky wasn't eating and I couldn't keep threatening to leave and still stay put. I had it out with her a week later, after an evening of watching her chop up all her food as small as she could, then, as if I wouldn't notice, hide it under a lettuce leaf. The next morning, I went at her. All brass and bugles blaring, that's me. But it was no use, she just curled into herself, didn't say a word. Absent while present, if you get my drift. I was so angry I had to leave the house. Slammed the front door shut, felt like a right turnip. Mum always slammed the door when she was losing an argument. And, hello, here I was doing the same thing. I regretted it the second I started to walk away from the cottage. I shouldn't have called her a spoilt bitch. Never should have said that. I thought when I returned she'd most probably suggest that me and my big mouth catch a train to London.

I went for a long walk to calm down. I considered all my options and none of them looked that rosy. If I stayed and Becky didn't eat, I would be blamed. If I left and Becky didn't eat, I would be blamed. I definitely wasn't holding the Willy Wonka golden ticket, that's for shizzle. I was munching on all this in my head when I noticed Mark driving past in his van. I remember thinking, how boring, he just has 'Mark Keele Chimney Sweep' written on the side. I reckoned it should have said 'Mark Keele, the Cleanest Chimney Sweep in Suffolk'. He waved at me and I didn't wave back. This nursery-rhyme village was beginning to give me the willies.

'Hello.'

I looked up to see this woman, a woman I had never met before, smiling at me as if she'd known me all her life.

'You're staying at the Burns house,' she said.

'Yes,' I said, slightly aggressively because it was no one's business where I was staying.

But Mrs Sunshine with her straw shopping basket bobbing with vegetables took no notice. She had a smile glued to her face, the one the Jehovah's Witnesses wear when they knock on our front door. A sort of martyred expression, as if to say, whatever the world throws at me, I will smile.

'I'm so glad that Becky isn't there alone,' said Mrs Sunshine. 'She needs a friend. If there's anything you want, just call on me – everyone knows where I live.'

Mrs Sunshine said her name and it went in one ear and drained out before reaching the other.

I walked away and tried to figure out how she knew that I was staying at the Burnses'. But then, when I looked at all the cottages around me, I could see their windows listening, their loose-tongued curtains flapping. It gave me the heebie-jeebies, made me long for the silver-foil lights of the high-rises in London.

It started to rain – that thin summer rain that is more of a mist. I went back to face Becky, certain I'd see my rucksack packed and waiting in the hall. Instead, I saw Becky sitting cross-legged on the window seat in the kitchen, writing in her Moleskine. She closed it when she saw me. I thought, here it comes: 'Pack your jim-jams and bugger off.'

She said, 'Tomorrow, will you come with me to the open prison?'

That was the thing about Becky. You never knew what she was going to say. She hopscotched over conversations you were having and returned to them when you'd forgotten what you'd been talking about. It kept you on your toes.

'Why?'

'Because there is someone there I want to interview.'

I was pretty sure it had to be Icarus. I couldn't think who else Becky would be interested in.

I said, 'Is it him?'

Becky nodded and went back to the Moleskine.

I didn't get it and said so.

She looked at me with a sad sort of expression as if to say, I doubt if you'll ever get it, Jazmin. But she didn't say that. I thought it, but she didn't say it.

What she did say was, 'I have an idea for my next book.'

'Becky,' I said, 'you can't just walk into an open prison and say, "Hi, I would like to see this man called Icarus." They won't let you in. For open, read shut.'

Becky had that lazy smile on her face, the one that told you she'd already managed the impossible.

'I phoned Tess Renshaw.'

'Who?' I said, though I knew the answer. I just needed time to figure out my reply.

Tess Renshaw was Becky's editor. It turned out that she was all friendly with a man who worked with the Home Secretary. Job done. Permission granted. Tomorrow at eleven o'clock.

I sat down, defeated. Talk about being wrong-footed.

I just said, 'Will you eat something if I make it?'

Becky shrugged. 'I'll try.'

But when I leapt up to go to the kitchen, she said, 'Tomorrow.'

I had no wish to climb onto the same merry-go-round that I'd just managed to climb off. Look, if she wanted to starve, that wasn't my problem, was it?

Chapter Five

I don't know how helpful all this is to you. Perhaps it's a bit too much information. Are you recording what I'm saying? Because you haven't taken any notes.

You must have a good memory – that's a rarity these days. Go on, show me how good your memory is.

You remembered every word. That's ruddy phenomenal.

It's strange. I haven't spoken about this to anyone before – well, no one who wasn't involved in it – because no one has ever understood what really happened. After the inquest someone suggested that I see a psychiatrist. I couldn't face looking at another person who believed that I was telling fairy stories. You're not like that, Mr Jones. You listen. Two rare qualities, listening and memory. Back then, no one was silent long enough to hear their own breath, let alone what I had to say.

I suppose you want to know what happened when we went to the open prison to meet Icarus. All right. If I tell you, would you answer one of my questions?

Chapter Six

Tess Renshaw. She drove an Audi, one that made me think of a cockroach on wheels and only had two seats. Two seats. Just hold that image because if you take me, Becky and, of course, Tess, that makes three. Me being the 'does she have to come?' girl, I sat scrunched up in the back while Tess drove us to the prison and did all the talking. I lay there and watched the sunlight play on the trees – you know, that golden summer light when the days are long and carefree? The carefree bit is a joke. Becky drew with her finger on the window and I don't think she listened to a word.

Tess has a motormouth. Tess said she had the most exciting piece of news: this really hot actor was to play the lead in the film of *The Martian Winter*. Becky didn't stop drawing.

'I don't know who he is,' she said.

Tess laughed. She laughed not because something was funny, but because she wasn't sure if she was dealing with a mad girl.

Still Becky said nothing. Tess changed the subject. Her voice was a tad more serious, talking about the open prison and about Icarus.

'He was nineteen when he was convicted so he would now be about forty or forty-one,' she said.

'Too old to be of interest to you, Becks,' I piped up.

Becky giggled.

Tess let out an exasperated sigh.

'I hope, Jazmin, that we're going to be grown-up about this. It took quite some arranging.' Tess answered her hands-free. 'No, darling,' she said to who knew who. 'That's my final offer.' Click. Gone is the speaker. Through gritted lipstick she muttered, 'Agents.'

I felt Becky's hand find mine and give it a squeeze.

How much wire fencing does an open prison need? Open? No. Though the word 'prison' describes the dump very well. We went through one clanking door after another until we reached a waiting room. The place smelled of disinfectant and sweat. I sat on a green plastic bench while Tess and Becky went to see Icarus. Two minutes later – maybe three – all right, five – out comes Tess on the war path, deploying her weapon of mass destruction.

'Is this some kind of joke, Henry?' she said into her mobile. 'Becky Burns wanted to see Icarus, not some nineteen-year-old drug dealer.'

I couldn't hear what was being said by Henry but before he was nuked into tomorrow Tess marginally calmed down. Her voice pivoted on the see-saw of believing and not believing. She came down on the side of not believing. From the bass note of Henry's voice I got the impression that jokes weren't his thing. Tess glanced at me, an irritated 'I could do without you, cow' kind of look, and walked into the corner of the waiting room near a water cooler. The rest of the conversation was inaudible.

Finally, she knocked on the door that she had stormed out of and the guard opened it – not to let her in but to let Becky out.

'Becky, darling,' said Tess, 'there's been some terrible mistake but I can put it right.'

'There's been no mistake,' said Becky. 'I want to leave now.'

Tess looked at her watch. She was calculating exactly how many minutes the visit had lasted, weighed up against how many things she had to promise Henry, on top of how many hours she had driven. Before she could announce the solution to the equation, her phone rang.

'Yes. Um – yes, all right. Tell her I can make the meeting.'

Tess turned to us.

'Let's be going,' she said, artificially bright. 'I'll take you home.'

'No,' said Becky. 'I want to go into Woodbridge, I'm starving.'

'Good,' said Tess, the LED bulb of her expression waning.

Once in the safety of her Audi, she said, 'Look, I really need to be back in London. Would you girls be all right if I dropped you off? This has all been a bit of a fiasco. I will see what I can do about you meeting the actual Icarus. Henry must take me for a fool.'

I couldn't imagine anyone thinking such a lightweight thought about her.

'I want to go to Woodbridge,' Becky said again. 'To The Crown.'

'I'm so sorry, darling – I can't stay for lunch,' said Tess.

'That's OK,' said Becky.

Too true it was OK.

'We need money for lunch,' I said, 'and for the minicab to take us home afterwards.'

Becky might be away with the fairies but someone has to have their feet on the ground.

'No probs,' said Tess.

I could see what she was thinking. A strategic withdrawal. Fall back and regroup. We whizzed along far too fast and Tess had to brake really hard near the airbase as three deer crossed our path.

'Damn,' she said, genuinely shocked. 'I didn't see them. Are you all right, darling?' she asked Becky.

Perhaps she should have thought of that before putting her foot on the accelerator. Or did she think all those 'beware of deer' signs were there to decorate the road?

Three more deer made a bolt for it and I wondered if they had just waited to see whether we or their mates would be dead meat.

I felt like a bent plastic doll by the time I climbed out of the car and glad that I wouldn't have to go back to Orford in it.

Tess gave me a fifty-pound note. I did my not-impressed look and she handed me another.

'I want the receipts,' she said.

Then, enjoying the admiring looks her car was getting, she stepped on the gas, as they say in films, and disappeared in a haze of speed in a twenty-miles-per-hour zone.

I wasn't for one minute expecting to actually have lunch in

The Crown, but Becky walked in and asked for a table for three.

'Who's the third?' I asked.

'Alex. I texted him.'

We sat at a table with white linen napkins and a lot of cutlery. And I felt a right prat. I had never in all my life eaten at a restaurant. McD's, yes. This, never.

'Tess said you hadn't seen Icarus, that it was some drug dealer who looked like him. That you'd been conned.'

Becky had her head down, staring at the menu.

'I wasn't conned,' she said. 'It was Icarus.'

'You sure, Becky?'

'Yes. Double, treble sure. He saw the knots in me.'

'Knots?' I repeated. 'What does that mean?'

'The knots in my head,' she said, looking up at me. 'You know, when he smiled at me it was as if I'd got off a train and he was there waiting for me.'

'Come on, explain.'

'You'll laugh.'

I didn't think I would. I wasn't finding any of this funny, far from it. If I was honest, it was beginning to spook me a bit.

'Go on,' I said.

'He untangled me.'

'Wait. Hold on. You saw this nineteen-year-old guy who can't be Icarus because time doesn't stop and no one remains young for ever, apart from Peter Pan – you saw him for ten minutes and he messed with your brain? Becks, you were conned.'

'You're right, no human stays nineteen. And no, and no again, I wasn't conned. I'm not stupid.'

I could see me going off on one and it all turning ugly, so I said, 'No, you're not. So what is this Icarus, an alien?'

'I don't know. Maybe, yes. All I know is that he is probably the most perceptive person I've ever met.' She changed the subject. 'What do you want to eat? I feel empty, as if I haven't eaten for weeks.'

'Surprise, surprise: you haven't.'

Becky ordered the fish and chips and non-alcoholic cocktails for both of us. She ordered as if she was as hungry as me.

'What about your friend?' said the waitress, nodding at the empty place.

'Oh, yes,' said Becky. 'Make that three fish and chips – and three prawn cocktails to start.'

I was speechless. This was a girl who ate air and was full. I didn't believe she would eat any of it. But never mind – I was bloody famished.

The waitress put bread and a saucer of olive oil on the table. Becky dipped the bread in the oil and ate it.

I was waiting – for what, I didn't know – when I heard Alex's voice.

'Hi, Jazmin – good to see you.'

'I ordered,' said Becky, olive oil running down her chin.

'You're eating,' said Alex.

'Yes.'

The first course came and I was surprised that Becky ate every prawn and every shred of lettuce.

'So what was Icarus like?' asked Alex. 'Wizened and out of touch?'

'No – not in the least.'

She stood up and went to the loo. I thought I knew what she was about to do.

Alex said, 'Jaz, what happened this morning in that prison?'

'I don't really know. Becky said that Icarus untangled her.'

'Untangled her? Is she totally losing it?'

I wasn't really concentrating on what Alex was saying as I was thinking about Becky, that now she would be chucking up in the toilet. I could see Alex was thinking the same and was just talking for the sake of it because it was better than thinking about Becky and vomit. But only two minutes later Becky was back, all smiles. OK. How long does food need to be in your stomach before your body starts to use it? Maybe she'll wait until after she's had her fish and chips.

But she was still sitting there, eating, talking, and I was gobsmacked when she ordered pudding. I couldn't eat another thing. Becky appeared to be on a mission to eat every pudding on the menu.

She'd got through cheesecake, sticky toffee pudding and tiramisu, and was asking about ice cream when Alex said, 'Becky, you'll be sick if you keep eating – or is that the plan?'

'I'm just hungry,' she said.

'OK,' said Alex, less and less convinced. 'What happened to make you decide to eat?'

'Icarus,' said Becky. 'He took the pain away.'

'Becky, come on, he's a fantasist. He's playing with you.'

'He's not. Anyway,' said Becky, 'I think you will like him. You'll meet him tonight.'

'Is that a joke?' said Alex.

Becky looked at him through her curtain of hair.

I felt ill. I could tell she was deadly serious.

'No,' she said.

'How?' said Alex.

Becky didn't bother with 'how'.

'In The Jolly Sailor at eight.'

'Yeah.' Alex looked exasperated. 'Whatever . . .'

I said, 'Becky, Icarus is in prison and . . .'

Becky licked her spoon.

Alex rang for a minicab to take us to Orford, but Becky wanted to go to Saxmundham first and stop at the supermarket because there was nothing to eat at home.

I stayed in the cab while Alex went to help his sister with the shopping.

The minicab driver had a big, hairy head and the rest of him seemed welded into his plastic car-seat cover.

'You know who I had in my cab last week?' he piped up. 'Only that Rex Muller.'

'I don't know who Rex Muller is,' I said.

'Yeah, you do – the famous artist. The one who did the portrait of that Icarus. Y'know, it was shown a few years back, up in London. They say it caused people to have hallucinations. Had to be taken down. Rex Muller,' he said again, as if repeating the name would make it clearer. 'It was his brother and his girlfriend who that Icarus pushed off St Paul's.'

I suddenly had an urge to leave Suffolk, to walk away from all this weird shit and catch a train back to London. I'd got out of the car and was heading towards the car park exit when I heard Alex call me.

'Jaz! Jazmin, where're you going?'

Chapter Seven

If Alex hadn't called my name in that car park I most probably would have caught the train and gone home – the path not taken. I've had long enough to think how different it all would have been. That's the thing about paths: you stumble across them, decide which one to take, knowing you'll never find the other one again. At school I had an English teacher, Mr Abel. He was very keen on the poetry of Robert Frost. You know – the two roads diverging in a yellow wood? I never understood it back then when the world seemed a spaghetti junction of roads to take. But now I think I do understand what he was on about. The road I took did make all the difference.

It was the sight of Becky with a supermarket trolley full of food that could have fed the five thousand that stopped me – that and the woebegone expression on Alex's face. It screamed, 'Don't leave me here, I don't know what to do.' So I turned round. It sounds dramatic, but I knew then that I was stuck there, for better or worse.

The minicab driver unglued himself from his plastic seat

and reluctantly helped fill the boot. We couldn't fit it all in and we had to sit squashed up between all the groceries, Alex in the front, Becky silent in the back with me.

Come to think of it, we were all quiet, except for the minicab driver. Another captive audience and, on his chest, stuff that needed to be got off it. 'I was telling your friend here,' he said to the rear-view mirror, 'I was telling her about the artist, the famous one with the painting that was shown up in London.'

Alex said, 'I'm sorry, I don't know what you're talking about.'

I could see that detail wasn't going to stop the minicab driver; it just gave him the opportunity to say all over again what he'd said to me.

'Rex Muller,' said Alex.

'That's him,' said the minicab driver.

'Rex Muller?' repeated Becky, coming out of her trance. 'His work is amazing – he did that album cover for the Megabytes. You say he was Lazarus's brother?'

'That's the one,' said the driver. 'But he didn't paint his brother, he painted Icarus.'

I wanted to say, 'Shut it, gobshite,' but I knew he wouldn't. He changed gear and waited for us to be impressed. The drive from Saxmundham to Orford was going to be long enough for him to puke it all out. Becky was wide awake.

'Wait,' she said, when she realised that she hadn't been listening properly. 'Start again.'

She pulled her feet up onto the seat and stared at the back of the driver's hairy head.

'It was the summer after Icarus pushed Lazarus and his girlfriend off St Paul's,' said the driver.

'What was?' said Alex, irritated. 'What are you on about about?'

'Quiet,' said Becky, then to the driver, 'Just tell us.'

'The painting was shown at the exhibition, and this lady came from Somerset for the day to see it. The painting was called *Icarus Falling*. Though he wasn't, not in the painting: he was standing upright. Didn't have wings. The lady collapsed in front of it. She was taken to hospital – dead the next day.'

'How old was this lady?' said Alex.

'In her eighties,' said the minicab driver.

'It was probably just a coincidence,' said Alex. 'Nothing to do with the painting.'

'That's what you think,' said the driver. 'The next day, two other people collapsed – and they weren't old.'

'And did they die?' said Alex.

'No. Not that I remember.'

'And how many people saw the painting and didn't collapse?'

'I don't know,' said the minicab driver. 'All I know is what I read in the *Sun*. Three weeks later, five people had been taken to hospital, complaining of visions.'

Alex sighed. 'Is that it? Sounds to me like mass hysteria. If you've finished, could you turn on the radio?'

Becky said, 'No – go on – I'm interested.'

'Then there was that school party. All the kids collapsed in front of the painting.'

'Did they die?' said Alex.

'No, but they were in hospital, comatose, for ten days. When they came round they all said they'd had dreadful headaches the minute they looked into Icarus's eyes. That's what did it.'

'Did what?' said Alex.

'They saw another world,' said Becky. 'And it blew their minds.'

I was in the worst mood by the time we arrived back at the cottage, and that grub of a minicab driver tried to overcharge us by goodness knows how much. I was so pissed off, I was gagging for a fight. I didn't care how much he moaned on about distances and having to go back empty. I refused to pay him what he asked and slammed the car door.

Becky didn't unpack the food. She took a KitKat and said she wanted to do some writing. Alex had taken himself off upstairs to look up the Icarus painting on his dad's computer when the phone rang.

'Sorry to bother you, but is Alex there? It's his mum.'

I shouted up the stairs and put the phone down when I heard him lift the receiver.

I'd just about got everything put away when Alex came down.

'Do you want to go for a walk?' he said.

We walked for miles in silence until at last we stopped and sat on an upturned boat. Alex took my hand.

'Thank you,' he said.

'For what?' I said.

'For not leaving us – not leaving me.'

I tried to look casual and said, 'That's OK.'

To my surprise he kissed me.

I hadn't realised how much I needed that kiss or to feel his arms round me. At that moment the heavens opened. We might as well have been standing under a power shower. He pointed to a barn in the distance.

'Race you there,' he said.

We ran until we were out of the rain. We were soaking wet and, without thinking the wrong or right of it, he took off my top and I took off his.

Mr Jones, you don't need to know more.

That's a strange question. What did I feel? . . . Well, you know what it feels like when you're with someone you really fancy, don't you?

No, I wasn't in love with him then – no, that happened later. I was in lust. Come on, you've been there, haven't you? He was lovely, and we fitted together. Oh hell, how we fitted together. That afternoon, while Mother Nature gave us one of her more spectacular thunderstorms, he made love to me. It was bloody amazing. He wasn't like the other boys I'd been with – he was kind, caring, not embarrassed. Anyway, that's not what I was going to say. It's just what happened.

We'd forgotten about the time and had to make a bolt for The Jolly Sailor. By then the sun had come out and Orford was a picture-postcard pretty English village.

Becky was sitting in the pub garden with a packet of crisps and a shandy. I was so relieved to see just her sitting there and no sign of Icarus. All right, I was also relieved that she didn't ask where we'd been or why we'd been so long. I noticed that she was wearing make-up and looking good, even talking more than usual. By nine o'clock I was thinking about swallows – I don't see swallows in the city – and had forgotten the reason we were at the pub in the first place.

Then I saw him and everything stopped. Alex was in the middle of telling a joke and he too stopped before the punchline. Becky beamed and stood up.

'I knew he'd come,' she said.

He was tall, dark-haired, wore jeans, a white T-shirt and sunglasses. He looked like a film star. Everyone stared at him. There was no doubt it was Icarus: he looked like all the pictures I'd seen of him. I thought, those glasses aren't going to fool anyone.

'You came,' Becky said, her voice almost childlike.

'Of course – I said I would,' he said. 'Did you eat lunch?'

'Yes, I actually felt hungry.'

'Good. That's a start.'

I must have been staring at the two of them open-mouthed. He was talking to Becky as if he'd known her all her life.

'You're Jazmin,' he said. 'And Alex. Good to meet you both.'

'Do you do this a lot?' I asked.

'Do what?'

'Walk out of prison and go to the pub?'

'Sometimes,' he said.

'How?'

'I walk through the walls,' he said.

'Is that a joke?' I said.

'Drink?' he asked.

'Yes,' I said. What was he going to do – go to the bar where

47

surely he'd be recognised straight away? 'Yes,' I said again.

Becky smiled at me as he went in. 'You think he'll be recognised?'

'Yes. Double yes and yes again.'

'No and no and no. Because Icarus would be about forty-two.'

She had a point.

'Then who is he?' I asked.

'Icarus,' she said.

He came back with the drinks, said he'd ordered food, then sat next to Becky and began to talk to her. I watched them – Alex and me both watched them. This is the thing, Mr Jones: there was something very genuine about Icarus. Becky talked to him in a way she didn't talk to us. He understood, he listened. And all that was vulnerable in her seemed to be held in his gaze. And I felt that she did the same for him. Alex's hand found mine under the table and squeezed it. I sort of forgot about what Icarus was supposed to have done and all the crazy shit from the minicab driver. You know, sometimes you have to enjoy what you have. No point fighting it, I told myself. Whatever this was, Becky had that look on her face, one that told you she'd inherited the earth.

I don't believe in love at first sight. I definitely believe in lust at first sight – but not love. But by the end of the evening at the pub, I wasn't so sure. Alex whispered to me he would see Icarus back to the prison – if that was where he wanted to go. Icarus kissed Becky. It felt weird, I didn't know what to think. Alex and me stood there like a couple of plum puddings.

When we returned to the house, Becky put her bag on the table and sticking out of it was an exercise book. I hadn't seen it before. Quickly, she snatched her bag away.

'Where did you get that exercise book from?'

As I asked the question I knew the answer.

'It's private,' she said.

'Show it to me.'

'Icarus gave it to me to look at.'

'Why? Why would he do that? He hardly knows you.'

'You don't understand.'

Not a truer word had been said all evening as far as I was concerned.

'No,' I said, 'I don't. He is very handsome but – I don't know if he isn't a con artist.'

'You are so wrong.' Becky twiddled her hair, then said, 'When I visited Icarus in prison, he looked at me and I felt he saw me – all of me.'

'What does that mean? I see you – all of you.'

'You see what you want to see. Everyone wants me to be someone else.'

'You think I'm the same as everyone?'

'Yes. No – sort of . . . no, I can't explain.'

'You can. You're the one who's good with words – give it a go.'

'Ruth sees me as her clever daughter; Simon as a feather in his cap; Tess as someone to make money out of.'

'And me?'

She picked up her bag and moved away but I was faster and stronger. I'd been the eater, remember. I took the exercise book and opened it. The paper was squared, the kind Becky liked to write on in her Moleskine notebooks, but the writing was all double-Martian as far as I was concerned. I handed it back to her.

'Do you understand it?'

'No,' she said quickly.

I knew she was lying.

I felt so angry. Angry at myself, at Becky, at this so-called Icarus. All right, if I was honest, I felt really stupid that I'd had sex with Alex. The bloody notebooks were the cherry on the whole cow-turd of a cake.

I went upstairs and turned on Simon's computer. I googled 'Icarus notebooks'.

There were, according to Wikipedia, twenty notebooks belonging to Icarus. Every code-breaker in the world had tried to decode them. Not one of them had had any success. It was then that I began to have a terrible feeling that this guy was no con artist but the real McCoy.

Chapter Eight

That's not fair, Mr Jones; I've told you about Icarus. You said you'd answer one question.

What if this is the end of my story – what if I stop now? What then?

All right, but I want to have the chance to ask you a few things. Is that a deal?

Look, Mr Jones, Becky could have been cooking up porkies when she told me later that she understood those scribbles. She'd only translated fragments and when they were shown to her editor, Tess, at the inquest, she said she thought they were notes Becky had made for her next novel.

I'll get them. You can see for yourself.

Troyon did not survive the impact. Ishmael has been taken. I have left stones. I will attempt to penetrate the citadel.

Skye and Lazarus are more like us than humans. I don't tell Phoebe for I can see she loves the girl.

This emotion called love. It is wrapped up in time, measured by years. The more I see of humans the more complicated love becomes. It is not an exchange of goods. It has no price, it is not a simple connection to other beings. Love is much deeper, its tendrils reach into the bad and the good in humans. I don't believe we should give up on this project. I cannot return until I learn how to love.

It was a mistake that should never have happened. I have sent back a girl made of clay and a boy risen from the dead. I see now that what I thought was their love for each other was but a call to go home.

Her name is Becky Burns. Too thin, in her head knots of loneliness threaded with fear of love, fear of life. In her eyes I see me. She asked me if her mind was her own. I undid one simple knot. To live she must eat.

That's all, Mr Jones, that's all I have. There may be more, somewhere.

Chapter Nine

Alex didn't come back that night, nor the following morning. I tried to text him but I couldn't get a signal on my phone, not even in the bathroom. I was dead worried. What if they hadn't gone to the prison and Icarus had kidnapped him and pushed him off the battlements of Orford Castle? I hardly slept that night. I tossed and turned and told myself I'd been a right muppet and should never have let what happened with Alex happen, should have played harder to get, not been such a pushover. Should have, would have, could have; should have had a bit more confidence in myself but I didn't.

In the morning, Miss Becky, all fresh as a flower, said, 'Did you sleep well?'

'No,' I said. 'I must have slept on Cloud Three, it's very uncomfortable. I see Cloud Nine was taken.'

'Do you want some?' said Becky, taking yogurt from the fridge.

'No, I just want to know if Alex is all right. Have you heard anything?'

'Alex's phone is broken,' she said. 'He sent me a text this

morning from his mum's phone. He says he'll get his mended in Woodbridge.'

'That's all?'

Becky looked suprised. 'What more should there be?'

'That someone noticed Icarus was gone from the prison? Or do they give you the key to the door once you've been banged up for twenty-three years?'

'You still don't believe it's him, do you?' she said with a smile. 'I told you before, you're wrong. He's extraordinary.'

I couldn't eat a thing. I nursed a cup of coffee, listening to Becky rhythmically chewing muesli. I still couldn't get my head around Becky eating and the noise of it began to grate on me. I realised I was way out of my depth. She needed some parental care and I thought I should maybe call Ruth. I took out my phone and went upstairs.

I was also half hoping there'd be a message from Alex. Nothing. Why had I been so hasty? I hadn't even asked him if he had a girlfriend. I wished then that I'd taken the path that led to the train and London. I knew I'd made an idiot of myself and now I was lost in the yellow woods and it wasn't pretty. It was the normal shitty place I always found myself in. I'd been there before – and without protection. At least Alex had been prepared.

Stop thinking about it. Just stop it. All right, girl, you've blown it, but so what? You have the right, and if the mood takes you . . . and all that drivel. The idea of calling Ruth went out of my head.

I sat down at Simon's computer. I wanted to find out more about the painting. There was this group of people who had all been affected by it and blogged about the visions that they still had. It made good reading.

Last night I saw the hologram horse again, pulling a wheel-less carriage …

Enough. That's enough. I was about to tap the sleep keys when a message flashed on the screen. It was from her of the two-seater Audi fame and I thought it must be for Becky. I read it so I could tell Becky what it said. I read it once and it made no sense. I read it again and it made perfect sense.

Darling Fish Face
I've managed to wangle a weekend. Booked Paris, the usual hotel. Have you done the deed?
Love you.

It disappeared, the brazen blush of words, and wasn't to be found in the inbox but if you went to the archive the whole sordid affair glowed back at you. The last one, from Simon, made it quite clear what was coming our way, and coming today. I quickly closed down the computer, washed up the coffee mugs, found the Hoover and came over all Mary Poppins until the place was spick and span. I thought about lunch, then decided it would be pointless as no one would eat anything after Simon had dropped an atom bomb with the power to blow the Burnses' lives into a divorce court.

He arrived in his Aston Martin, wearing a tweed suit that wasn't meant to be worn in the country, having more to do with urban foxes than with country cow shit.

'Jazmin,' said Simon. 'I'm so pleased to see you.'

I could see that thinly concealed under his smile was 'please get lost so that I can speak to Becky alone'.

'Wow,' he said, artificially bright. 'Wow, how tidy it all is. Amazing. Well done.'

Becky came into the kitchen, still not dressed.

'What are you doing here, Dad?'

'Come to see my princess.'

I thought to myself, I won't tell her that Tess Renshaw calls him Fish Face. Though come to think of it, there is something a tad coddish about him.

I called goodbye and set off for a walk in the rain. I can hardly remember the sun shining that summer. It must have done, but not in my memory.

I was heading towards the harbour when I bumped into Mrs Sunshine again, the basket still stuck to her arm, this time full of bread. She was holding an umbrella with Monet's water lilies on it.

'Ah, just the person I wanted to see.'

Now, I would have liked to have stopped her right there and asked her why she wanted to see me. Was it on account of my dreads, or the tattoo on my right arm, or possibly something to do with the six piercings in my ear?

Turned out it was to do with a woman I had never heard of before that day. They kept coming out of the woodwork. Mrs Berry.

'I thought,' said Mrs Sunshine, 'that Becky should take the Doulton figurines Mrs Berry promised her before her cottage is cleared and everything is taken to auction.'

'I don't understand,' I said.

She smiled a smile that said, 'Why should you? You are definitely not one of us.' I thought then that maybe the whole village was teeming with aliens and I was the only human left.

'Just tell Becky that they will be there Friday. She'll understand. Must dash.'

An hour later, I was walking slowly back to the cottage, hoping I'd left it long enough, when Simon's car came towards me and stopped.

'Jazmin,' he said, winding the window down and leaning across the front seat to look up at me. 'Thank you for all you're doing.' He hesitated, then said, 'Ruth has gone to India for the summer, to do a yoga course. I would like you to keep an eye on Becky. Don't leave her, will you? Here . . .' He took an envelope from his pocket. 'This is for you.'

I have been broke since once upon a time. I took the envelope. I knew what money felt like.

'Thanks,' I said. 'But, Simon, I want to talk to you . . .'

He already had the car in gear. He couldn't get out of there fast enough. I watched Fish Face do a three-point turn that would have embarrassed James Bond, before shooting out of Orford, heading for the bright lights of Paris.

I stopped in the bus shelter and looked in the envelope. Two thousand pounds. Unbelievable. Two thousand pounds to wash his conscience clean.

I returned to the cottage, wondering what state I'd find Becky in. Please, I thought, please, may she not stop eating.

Chapter Ten

Who tells the truth? Does my mother? Did my father? Do you, Mr Jones? I don't think there is any truth to be had in this world. That's why we're all so screwed up.

I've been talking for ages and still we're not anywhere near the reason you've come to speak to me.

Funny, but I've found it comforting, talking to you and not being judged. Do you mind me asking – who will you be interviewing next?

That'll be interesting. He came to see me before the inquest to tell me it would be best if I didn't say too much in court. He was right. I should've listened. I hoped he would answer a few questions for me but he didn't. He's a quiet man.

Shall I carry on?

Chapter Eleven

Becky was sitting at the kitchen table, studying Icarus's exercise book.

'I've just seen Simon,' I said. 'Are you all right, Becks?'

'This house, and the house in London, are built on lies,' she said. 'Lies are bricks that the truth slowly moulders away until the house falls down. Simon said that he had only stayed with Ruth because of me.'

'That's terrible,' I said.

'He's moving to New York.'

'Does Alex know?'

I'd never seen Becky this furious. Tears were pricking the corners of her eyes.

'Simon's on his way to see him now.'

'New York?' I said. 'Why New York?'

'I suppose he wants a lot of water separating him from Ruth so she can't grab hold of him with her mermaid claws and drag him to the bottom of the briny sea. And he's been headhunted by a top firm of architects there.'

'What about Tess?'

'Moving to New York too. Great. I've lost my dad and my editor.'

'You haven't lost them, you've just . . .'

'I don't care,' she said. 'It doesn't matter. I'm not going to be around. When they all hit the ground in pieces, I'll be well gone.'

I was going to ask her what she meant but as she was on the verge of tears, I thought better of it.

I said, 'It might all work out. You know, parents go through these crises and get back together again.'

'Where does that happen then?' Becky went to the fridge and took out a carton of half a dozen eggs and put it on the butcher's block. 'In some happy-clappy, soupy –' she lifted her fist and brought it down hard on the carton – 'film?' Eggs cracking, yolk spilling. 'Want an omelette?'

She poured the whole sorry mess into a bowl.

I'd helped her extract most of the eggshell when the phone rang. I picked it up and almost put it down again, the sobbing was so loud.

'Jazmin,' whimpered Ruth. 'Can I . . . can I speak to Becky?'

Becky looked at me. I mouthed 'Ruth' and she took the phone and put it on speaker.

'How could he?' Ruth shrieked. 'How could he do this to us, darling? And with your editor. How did he even meet her? The bitch!' There was a pause, then Ruth shouted, 'No! I'm talking to my daughter. I don't care if this is the first-class lounge, I won't be quiet.'

'Mum,' said Becky, 'Mum – Ruth – where are you?'

A man's voice came on the phone. 'This is the manager of the British Airways first-class lounge at Heathrow. I'm speaking to Mrs Burns's daughter? Your mother needs to calm herself and then she will call you back. Goodbye.'

'I suppose there was always a clue,' said Becky. 'Take away the M and it spells OTHER. Ruth is some other person, a mum I don't know.'

I put on Lou Reed and for no reason both of us sang, blasted it out loud and clear, and I wondered how many other less-than-perfect days were taking place behind the closed doors of Orford.

We sat down to eat and despite the eggshell the omelette tasted good.

'Do you think,' said Becky, 'that it would be better for all of us if there was no such thing as love? And definitely no passion?'

'That's a strange question.'

'Think about it. Love corrupts, passion ignites. Notice too that no country goes to war unless it feels passionately that God is on its side.'

'But there are many kinds of love,' I said.

'What if it didn't exist and there was just kindness? What if we were just kind and forgiving to one another? Then there would be no war. There would be no point.'

'And there wouldn't be art or music – hip hop or the Megabytes.'

Becky was about to say something when the phone rang again. We both stared at it and I hoped Becky wouldn't pick up, but it rang on and on until it became a siren. Becky answered it at last and pressed the speaker button. Ruth sounded really out of it.

'I'm so sorry, darling, so terribly sorry,' she said. 'I only found out today.'

'Where are you going, Mum?'

'Mumbai. I'm on the plane, waiting to take off. I'll call you when I get there. Don't worry, darling, it will all be fine.' The line crackled and an announcement could be heard telling passengers to turn off their mobile phones. 'I have to go to Mumbai, darling. You understand, I have to find inner peace.'

Another voice said, 'Please, Mrs Burns, you must switch off your phone now.' The line died.

'That illustrates the mother theory perfectly,' said Becky. 'She is just another loser exiled from the couple kingdom. Watch how fast your paper house burns down, Mrs Burns.'

She was silent. I was gobsmacked by Ruth's behaviour. I wouldn't have thought it of her, didn't see her as the run-away-and-hide kind of mum. I had imagined her coming down here to be with her daughter, not legless on a first-class flight to India. It made me wonder: who *is* grown-up these days?

'Just you and me then,' said Becky. 'I'm glad you're here, Jaz.' I went to put my arms round her. I felt guilty about the money but it didn't seem like a good time to tell her that her father thought he had to bribe me to stay with her.

'Grown-up. Stupid word, isn't it? I feel far more grown-up than my parents, don't you?'

'Yes, I do,' I said, and I told her about Mrs Sunshine and Mrs Berry but then had a feeling I was adding to all the sadness.

As far as I can remember, nothing much happened for a few

days. No Alex. No Icarus. Becky wrote in her Moleskine. Mum sent a postcard. Most unlike her. It had a picture of an old 73 bus on it. Said she was moving to a rented flat in Margate to be near Auntie Karen. It had a view of the sea and there was more than enough room for me. She even added that she was missing me. That made me smile. At least my mum seemed to be playing the slot machine of life and winning – if only pennies.

Simon emailed Becky saying that he would always love her.

'Bullshit,' said Becky. 'I hate him. And Ruth. At least you knew your mum was a messed-up cow pie. You weren't under any illusion that she'd always be there for you, no matter what. I'd been sold the whole "perfect family" package. Only it was long past its use-by date.' Her little bubble of anger burst. She said, in a small voice that I recognised from myself, the voice I use when my confidence has been eaten up, the voice that makes me feel six: 'I don't think Ruth cares about me at all.'

I could never have been an actor. I said, with as much conviction as I could muster, 'Of course Ruth loves you, she's your mum.'

But it sounded weak. Her loving mother was up a mountain with a guru and no internet connection. She did send one email, on the day she arrived. It was priceless that email, you couldn't have made it up. It went something like: 'When you are grown up, Becky, you will understand the pain I'm going through. And you will know why I had to leave.'

Ironic, really, because Becky never got the chance to grow up. Ruth got a chance to grow up and decided not to take it.

As my Auntie Karen would say, no one can agree on how many currants there should be in a bun.

On Wednesday, I said to Becky that I was going to catch the bus into Woodbridge and did she want anything. She didn't. What I couldn't tell her was that I was going to put a load of money into my savings account. I could've paid it in at the Post Office in the shop in Orford, but knowing how they all nattered I thought I didn't want news of my two thousand pounds spread, sticky as peanut butter, around the village.

I was nearing the town when my phone had a meltdown. Alex had texted about thirty times since I'd last seen him.

no i dont have a girlfriend

do you have a boyfriend

I want to see you

come on speak to me

give me a ring

ARE YOU IGNORING ME

On and on they went. My heart nearly flew out of my chest. The last texts were pretty pissed off because I hadn't answered. I texted him that my phone hadn't had any reception until I got to Woodbridge and he texted, straight away.

meet me by the cafe near the train station

I replied, saying I'd be there in fifteen minutes, but I spent thirty in the queue in the Post Office. I thought, why is everything so slow up here? In London, those old biddies going on about their roses to the man behind the counter would have been arrested for time-wasting.

I ran to the station and couldn't see Alex. Then there he was, coming towards me. I tried to look nonchalant. Like, so what? But I couldn't pull it off. I beamed at him.

He leaned over and kissed me, just like that.

'Where have you been?' I asked. 'Did Simon find you?'

'Message fifteen explained that I was staying with my mum because one of my kid brothers had chicken pox and Mum had to work. And yes, Simon did find me. And I don't want to talk about it.'

We walked along the river. We held hands and I became all girly and forgot that I'd ever been worried and wished that there were a hundred barns on the riverbank. Alex stopped by a Dutch barge.

'Do you want a drink?' he said.

'Yes,' I said.

'Good,' he said and hopped on the boat.

'Wait – I'm not doing breaking and entering.'

'You won't be,' said Alex. 'The boat belongs to Tom, my stepfather. This is where I live in the summer.'

It smelled of river and was much bigger inside than I thought it would be, with a table in the middle. Though to be honest, Mr Jones, I only became aware of all that later because one kiss led to another and another.

I asked Alex what had happened when he took Icarus back to the prison. He said the minicab had stopped near the gate, Icarus had got out, said goodbye and disappeared into the night.

'Do you think he went into the prison?' I asked.

'Maybe.'

I told him about the group of people who'd been affected by the painting of Icarus, and the visions they have to this day.

'You wouldn't believe it: hologram horses and wheel-less carriages.'

Alex said, 'Jaz – have you ever heard of the UFO sightings in Rendlesham Forest?'

'No. When was that, then?'

'Years ago. The time that Rex Muller's brother Luke died of meningitis and came back from the dead as Lazarus.'

'The Lazarus who Icarus pushed off St Paul's?'

'The same.'

I wasn't liking the sound of this but still I said, 'Tell me about the UFOs.'

'Mum remembers it, she was about fifteen at the time,' said Alex. 'The story was put about that a military plane had crashed in the forest near Bentwaters airbase. But strange lights were seen in the sky and rumours spread about UFO sightings. There was talk of aliens being taken from the craft. Military guys from the airbase went into the forest and against all the rules of keeping schtum they spoke out about what they saw.'

'Little green men?' I said.

'A UFO,' said Alex. 'And there were civilians who saw stuff too – a farmer in Eyke swore he saw a triangular spacecraft. And white oblong things falling from the sky. It was all denied and the Rendlesham Forest UFO Walk was set up so that the whole thing would look childish. But there are a lot of people around here who believe that something landed in the forest, something from another world. And many believe that the aliens are still here.'

'Do you think we could go back to kissing and cuddling?' I said. 'It feels safer.'

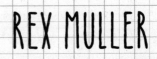
REX MULLER

Chapter Twelve

You're not, by any chance, about to write a book on Lazarus and Skye, or Icarus, are you, Mr Jones? Last time I went to Foyles there was a whole section on them. Completely crazy.

You want to talk about the meaning of love? That's original. But I don't quite see the connection with Icarus. The painting is of him, you know, not Lazarus.

I must apologise – I thought it would be best if we viewed the painting in the gallery. To be quite honest with you, no one has looked at it since it was shown at the Royal Academy. It's been in the gallery's warehouse ever since. There were postcards but even they caused problems. People complained of headaches. I never had any trouble when I was painting it.

I do appreciate that you've signed all the papers, it's just that if anything happens when you're looking at the painting, it's not my responsibility or the gallery's. Is that understood?

Perhaps you're right – keep your sunglasses on. I'll turn my back to it. I have no wish to see the painting again.

Icarus was nineteen when I did the portrait. The eyes I painted last because light troubled him and he had to wear dark glasses.

No, it was my suggestion that I paint him.

Why? That's a good question. I suppose because he reminded me of an eighteenth-century gentleman. He stood out, he didn't fit in. Come to think of it, neither did Lazarus or Skye.

Finished? Good. I know that you want to ask me a few questions but I would prefer to talk at my studio rather than here, if you don't mind. It's just round the corner.

I'm bad at dates . . . I must have met Icarus about a year before Lazarus and Skye jumped off the dome of St Paul's.

I don't know if they were in love. They were a strange couple, it's true, but then after Lazarus – you know he was my brother? My brother Luke? – after he rose from the dead he wasn't the same. But I never really believed this Lazarus was my brother.

Here we are. I told you it wasn't far. Let me find my keys . . . You're right, it's an amazing space. I moved in just after that Summer Exhibition. It was one of the worst times in my career – in my life. I thought what happened to all those people would mean that nobody would ever buy my paintings. Then I received a letter from a man I call Mr Invisible. He became my benefactor. He's never wanted to be named. All I know about him is that he likes my work. It's due to him that I have this studio.

It was Luke who was obsessed with UFOs and aliens. He had every book and magazine that he could lay his hands on. Yet after he was born again, so to speak, he never looked at them. To me, that was proof that Lazarus was not my brother, no matter what anyone said. And you see, Luke had blue eyes and

Lazarus's were black. Black as black. Black as Icarus's.

I thought it was Icarus you were interested in rather than Lazarus.

No, I don't mind talking about him, not now. It all seems to belong to another life. But I'm not good with words. Paint and colour are my language. Words can be read and misconstrued. In an image lies an undeniable truth.

Please sit down.

Chapter Thirteen

When I was fifteen we lived in a village called Eyke, outside Woodbridge, in a tumbledown house that my father was always in the process of doing up. Both my parents were teachers. Luke was younger than me by four years. I had trouble at school; he was the clever one. He used to do my homework for me. I loved him. If anyone said or did anything against him, they would have me to contend with.

A week before Christmas, Luke came home from school feeling unwell and two days later he was dead from meningitis. We had the tree, lights, decorations and Christmas cards full of cheer, but as for us – we'd run out of words. Words were inadequate, incapable of describing the grief we felt. The funeral was to be on 29th December.

That Christmas Day, we sat round the dining table wearing paper hats, staring at the turkey slowly congealing in its own fat. None of us ate a thing. The lights of the Christmas tree flashed until my dad couldn't stand it any more and unplugged them. We moved from the table to the sofa in the lounge and sat there, staring at the dead television. It stood next to the sideboard where the family photos were displayed. Blue-eyed Luke stared back at us. Time seemed to spin into infinity; it slipped past unnoticed until the room became dark and I could hear Mum softly crying. Dad took her up to bed.

I couldn't let all that wordless grief defeat me. I felt someone had to stay strong and, seeing how my parents were, I knew it wasn't going to be them. It must have been quite late and the house was in darkness when I took a torch and went outside. I remember seeing the red lights coming out of the sky. I tried to tell Mum and Dad about them the next day but their sadness was too thick a crust.

It was the night of the 27th that Mari, a friend from school, came to see me. Her father brought her over. He wanted to see if there was anything he could do. It was a bit awkward in the house with Mum and Dad stuck in a groove, so Mari and I went out to the garden. It was bitterly cold.

Then the lights were there again, dancing across the field opposite. We stood watching them, both of us memerised. Something about those lights made me feel that Luke was close to me. At one point a cloud seemed to come over us, blocking out the lights, and everything became dark. I realised I was looking up at the bottom of a huge craft hovering above our garden. We thought it must be from the airbase. But as we stood there, white objects began falling from it. One landed not far from us. It looked like a stone – white, oblong. Mari picked it up and handed it to me. I expected it to be hot but it was blood warm and unlike anything I'd ever touched before or since. She collected two more.

74

Mari said that perhaps the stone, that piece of unknown rock, could perform miracles. I was desperate for some comfort. That idea was easier to accept than the reality that Luke was dead. We were about to go back into the house when two military cars drove past. We slipped the stones into our pockets. Guilty treasures.

Mum was in a terrible state the following day. She said that Luke had to have his teddy bear, he couldn't be buried without it. She begged Dad to take it to the funeral parlour. She wasn't able to see her baby like that again.

Dad was just as fragile as her but nevertheless he did the manly thing. I said I'd go with him. We hardly spoke as we drove to Woodbridge. The funeral director greeted us and, to spare Dad, suggested that he put the teddy bear in the coffin himself.

It was only then that I knew what I was going to do. It was stupid, really, clinging to a stone, hoping for a Christmas miracle. I went with the funeral director to where Luke was lying in his coffin.

The funeral director asked if I was all right and I asked if I could have a moment by myself. He said he would be outside if I needed anything. When I saw Luke I knew he was dead, his body empty, his soul gone. I put the teddy in the coffin beside him. Under the teddy I put the stone. It was feather-light.

When we arrived home, Mum was sitting at the kitchen table with a man in a black suit. Another man, also in a black suit, was standing. Mum looked bewildered. They asked us questions, many questions. Had we seen anything out of the ordinary last night? Had we found anything unusual in our garden? Dad said no, Mum said she hadn't any idea what they were talking about. She said she hadn't seen any lights. The only person they didn't ask was me. Dad lost his temper and told them to get lost.

Early on the morning of the funeral, Mum was in the kitchen making egg sandwiches when the phone rang. She took the call and fainted, and when Dad picked up the receiver it looked as if he might go the same way. I took the phone off him and listened to the funeral director. He sounded pretty shaken. My brother Luke had returned from the dead. Dad phoned for a minicab to take them into Woodbridge. It was the wisest thing to do, as he didn't look as if he'd be safe behind a wheel. I stayed home, phoned people to tell them the funeral was off and waited. I ate a lot of egg sandwiches. By four it was dark, pitch black, and I lit the fire. At seven I called the police. They seemed surprised to hear from me and said that my parents had been taken with Luke to the military airbase and would be returning home soon.

It didn't make any sense.

The doorbell rang. I opened it to find a reporter asking me how it felt to have my brother back, a Lazarus risen from the dead.

I slammed the door and sat on the bottom step of the stairs, feeling guilty, feeling the stone had had something to do with the 'miracle'.

When I read what happened to that girl, Becky Burns, I was certain it was connected in some way to Lazarus and Skye. I never went forward to say so though, not after I had seen how the witnesses were treated at Icarus's trial.

I felt truly sorry for Jazmin Little. I went to see her. A lovely girl made into a scapegoat. I read that the lawyers pulled her statement to pieces. God knows how you carry on after that. They did the same to the poor man who had looked after Icarus in prison. I can't remember his name.

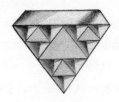

Chapter Fourteen

I knew that something was very wrong when the lights went off in the house and the telephone didn't work.

Our neighbour, Deirdre, came over. She'd heard the news about Luke and asked if I would like to go home with her until my parents returned. Deirdre and her husband Pete lived over the road and when we walked in, Pete was listening to the local radio.

'It's all over the news,' he said.

'What is?' I said. 'You mean Luke?'

'No,' said Pete. 'The UFO sightings in Rendlesham Forest. They've been denied, of course. The official story is that the lights people saw came from the lighthouse at Orford. Who's going to believe that?'

'Would you like something to eat, Rex?' said Deirdre.

'They've blocked off the lane,' said Pete. 'There's a black van parked at the bottom of the road and men in white boiler suits all over Mr Earle's farm. I spoke to him yesterday. He said that the UFO hovered over his field, good as landed in it. He saw it with his own two eyes. Then oblong things – white – fell from the sky. That's what those men are looking for. It's all going to be hushed up, you wait and see. They did it with Roswell, they'll do it with Rendlesham.'

Not for the first time that day I had the feeling that Luke's resurrection had something to do with that white stone. Much later I became convinced that everything that happened to Luke afterwards was my fault. I should never have put that stone in his coffin.

I was helping Deirdre in the kitchen when the headlights of two cars shone straight through the window. They pulled up outside my gate. For a moment I thought they'd brought my parents and Luke home but Deirdre and me watched silently as men in white boiler suits went into our house.

Mum, Dad and Luke returned the next day. I knew as soon as I went home that something wasn't right. The place was spotless in a way it had never been before. It made me want to scream. Put it back, make it all go back to how it was before Luke died.

My parents seemed disorientated, as if they had just woken from a deep sleep. Luke went to the fridge and opened and closed it, opened and closed it, opened and closed it. They all appeared to be in a trance. Although they *looked* like my mum, my dad, my brother, these three people were strangers to me. After that they had regular visits from a doctor – he wasn't our local GP. I wondered afterwards if it was the pills he prescribed that affected them so badly.

Mum had always been a great one for cuddles. She used to say that there was nothing that couldn't be cured by a good cuddle. Dad was the same – they were both touchy-feely. But after Luke came back they seemed surprised by any physical display of affection. A quizzical look would come over their faces as if they were trying to fathom why I would want to touch them.

Lazarus – I'll refer to him as Lazarus – was the most robotic of all. He looked like Luke but that was as far as it went. He would sit for hours in a dark room staring at nothing, not speaking, not moving. He gave me the creeps. I think it was because of Lazarus that Mari drifted away from me.

Lazarus went to school. Where Luke had been popular, Lazarus had no friends. I thought Mum and Dad might get better but they didn't. The doctor insisted that they kept taking the drugs, and he sent other medical people to help with Lazarus, who seemed incapable of coping in the world.

Yes, Mr Jones, you're right. That's enough for today.

MARI SCOTT

Chapter Fifteen

Rex called me last night. He said he'd chatted to you and found it helpful. Not a great one with words, is our Rex. But he said I was next on your list.

As we agreed, Mr Jones, I'm only going to talk about Phoebe and Skye, nothing else.

Anyway, why are you so interested in them? It always makes me laugh how the experts seem to know more about Lazarus and Skye than the people who actually knew them.

You must have got on well with Rex, Mr Jones – neither of you are very forthcoming.

I was at Ipswich shopping centre the other day, when this young woman came up to me and said she was doing a piece of art for the Civic Centre. It involved taking my picture and asking me what I'd wish for.

To begin with I said I wasn't interested but she was very persistent and suddenly I felt myself on the brink of tears.

I said, 'I wish I'd never picked up those stones.'

She said, 'That's original.'

I said, 'It's a bloody tragedy.'

She didn't take my picture. No doubt she thought I was a nutter. She found a chap with a Zimmer frame and asked him the same question – he said he wished his dog hadn't died.

Rex and I grew up in the same village. He was always an awkward boy. I suppose I really got to know him when we went to the same comprehensive school in Ipswich. We were joint top of our class in art and discovered we both had the same dream of going to art school in London. But I knew early on that he would be a better artist than me.

Why? It was because of a book he'd found, it was on the work of Rothko. I preferred Modigliani. Rex said when he looked at Rothko's last paintings they spoke of the thickening of blood. He didn't know anything about Rothko's life or death, not then. Rothko had committed suicide in 1970 and was found in a pool of his own blood – as rich and dark as his paintings. But you're not here to ask about Rex – you want to know about Skye and Lazarus.

Are you sitting comfortably, Mr Jones? Then I'll begin.

I met Phoebe Berry, Skye's mother, when I was fifteen. I'd never met a proper artist until then. She had gone to the same dump of a school that Rex and me attended. She was a bit of a legend in the art department – the girl done good. Her work had been shown in a gallery in Bond Street, and she taught at the Royal College of Art. Phoebe came to our school to give a lecture and have a look at all our work. She was very interested in Rex's and mine and told us we had talent. Neither of us had ever been told we were anything special. She invited us to visit her at her studio in Shingle Street. Do you know it? It's a row of little cottages on a pebble beach.

We cycled there. It was a hot day, I remember. Rex went all quiet when he saw Phoebe's studio. It was built in a secret garden, back from the house and the beach – you wouldn't know it was there unless you'd been told. I thought to myself, this is the life I want. Rex was so overawed, he didn't say anything. I managed to talk my way into a summer job. Rex was livid with me.

I pointed out as we cycled home that he already had a summer job in a second-hand bookshop and, anyway, I was going to be nothing more than a glorified dogsbody. He forgave me in the end.

What I never told him was that it was the best summer I'd ever had. Phoebe was living with a marine engineer called Frank. To me, back then, it all seemed so alternative, so romantic, living on the edge, refusing to conform. My main job was to help with the cooking – the house was always full of people. Frank's brother seemed to be living there most of the time too. There was a long table in the front garden overlooking the shingle beach, and every evening all the seats round it would be taken by friends who were passing through, staying the night or had just turned up with a bottle of wine.

It was a time that now seems bathed in the light of dreams, when everything was possible, golden, before the dark.

I went back to school wishing I didn't have to. Then Phoebe phoned to tell me she was pregnant – she and Frank were over the moon. They'd been trying for a long time.

Once autumn term started, there was no time to cycle over to Shingle Street. In November Phoebe had a miscarriage. I didn't know whether or not I should go and see her. I couldn't think what to say to someone who had lost a baby. But all of that was overshadowed by Luke's death. I think that was the worst thing that had ever happened in our lives up to that point. He was such a lovely lad, full of laughter. His death was impossible to comprehend. If I'd no words to say to Phoebe, I definitely had no idea what to say to Rex. I saw him a couple of days after Christmas. We were in his garden when . . . oh, Rex told you. Then you know about the stones. Yes, I gave one to him, I kept one and, not knowing what to say to Phoebe, I gave the third stone to her.

She'd invited me for lunch the next day. I hadn't seen her for a while.

In her studio she showed me a clay sculpture of a little girl. It took my breath away, it was so perfect, so full of yearning. We went back to the house to eat and I was surprised that Frank wasn't there. Phoebe said he'd gone to see his mother, and his brother was working. But I had the feeling that things weren't right. I suppose I was too young to understand what the loss of a child can do to you, how it can make the solid walls of love crumble.

I gave her the stone. We drank elderflower wine and she told me how much she and Frank had longed to have children and that now she wasn't able to have any.

Before I left we went back to her studio in the secret garden. It was nearly dark. We placed mistletoe and the stone in the clay girl's outstretched hands. I turned to look back as we closed the studio door and I was certain I saw something glimmer behind

the glass. I told myself the elderflower wine was not as innocent as I'd thought. As I got on my bike, Phoebe said she wanted to see more of me, but I didn't hear from her. Some months later I was told that she and Frank had adopted a little girl.

Rex said he was sure his brother had risen from the dead because of the alien stone. He said he should never have put it in Luke's coffin. I thought that was a load of gobbledygook until I met Skye.

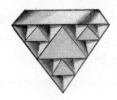

Chapter Sixteen

Phoebe had said she would help Rex and me prepare our portfolios. The trouble was, it was spring and we hadn't heard from her and it felt awkward to ask. I wanted to call her, but Rex said perhaps we should leave her alone. There was gossip about the little girl Phoebe and Frank had adopted – people said she was a strange one, she wasn't all there, had something wrong in the head.

One day I was walking in the woods near Rendlesham Forest. You know, Mr Jones, some of those trees are near as ancient as Britain itself. That was where I came across a girl of about eleven. She was standing in a clearing near a patch of burnt earth. She unnerved me, for there was no mistaking her likeness to the sculpture I had seen in Phoebe's studio. But I asked what her name was, and if she was all right.

She pointed up to the sky and said, 'I have to get home.'

It took ages – or rather, it seemed to take ages – to convince her that I could take her home.

She asked how I could do that and I said, 'By walking.'

'No,' she said. 'When I'm sixteen, I will jump.'

'You can jump now,' I said. 'There's nothing to stop you. You don't have to wait that long.'

She looked at me as if I was an idiot.

'I thought you understood,' she said. 'No one understands.'

I don't think she said anything more on the way home. I had younger brothers and sisters and if they'd got lost in the woods they would have been scared out of their socks, weeping and wailing and crying for Mummy. Not this little girl. She seemed much older than her years and, to be honest, not like a child at all. I wondered if Rex was right about the 'alien stones' and if in some way the stone was responsible. But I told myself over and over again, like a mantra, that it was impossible.

When we arrived at Shingle Street, Frank and Phoebe were frantic with worry. Phoebe ran towards Skye, arms outstretched. Skye just watched her. She didn't move, showed no emotion.

Phoebe was crying as she hugged Skye. Skye put her finger to the tears on Phoebe's cheek and tasted them. She said that they were salty, salty like the sea. She said, 'I don't have tears.'

Phoebe thanked me and I realised there was a way back to this life that I craved.

'If you need any help, I could babysit for you,' I said.

That's how I came to know Skye. And in return Phoebe helped me and Rex with our portfolios. As soon as Rex saw Skye he asked me if I'd given Phoebe one of the alien stones.

I said that they were just stones, ordinary stones, they had nothing to do with anything. But I didn't believe it. Rex didn't believe it. For both our sakes I stuck to my crumbling belief, too guilty to admit we'd played any part in what had happened. I wanted to get rid of my stone but I was worried that if I touched it, something bad might happen. So I left it where it was, in a metal money box at the bottom of my wardrobe.

I longed for Phoebe to confide in me about Skye, but she never did. I couldn't bring myself to ask what had happened to the sculpture of the little girl.

I would describe Skye as no more than an idea of a girl, an idea that was never going to flower. I looked after her all that summer and I refused to accept that a stone could have given life to clay.

Skye didn't like to run or swim, she never played, she just sat, watching the sea. She never ate, never slept. If she had been human she would have been dead. Put that in your book, Mr Jones.

Now, if this was a fairy tale I would tell you that Phoebe and Frank married and lived happily ever after. But this is no fairy tale.

I went to the Central School of Art to do a foundation course and Rex got a place at the Slade.

One day – it was May, the following year – Phoebe called to ask if I wouldn't mind looking after Skye for the night. She and Frank had a flat in Marylebone. I went there about six-thirty. I hadn't seen Phoebe for some time. She looked anxious. She apologised when I arrived – she didn't need me to babysit after all; Skye was insisting that she went home with her. I remember thinking that was strange: why wouldn't Phoebe want to take Skye back to Suffolk with her in the first place? I asked her what was going on.

Phoebe said it was nothing, that she wanted to take Frank out, a special evening, silly idea anyway. Then she asked if I would help her wrap a painting. It was a portrait of a man, quite beautifully painted in such a way that he seemed to be alive. He had such hypnotic eyes. I asked her who he was.

She said his name was Icarus.

I said, 'Like the man in the Greek myth who flew too close to the sun.'

Just then Skye came into the room. She said a barefooted man was looking for Icarus.

'I don't like the barefooted man,' she added.

I asked Phoebe what Skye was on about but all she would say was that she'd explain later.

'We have to go,' said Phoebe. 'It's getting late.'

Skye said, 'We're going to Granny's.'

I'd helped Phoebe out to the car with her bags and the painting when she said she'd forgotten something and went back into the flat.

I stood waiting with Skye and suddenly she said, 'You should say goodbye nicely. You won't see Phoebe again.'

I said, 'Skye, that's rubbish.'

'The future often is,' she said.

I was really irritated with her. Phoebe came rushing out and leapt into the car. I wanted to say something but all that came out was 'Take care.'

No one knows quite what happened. It was a terrible shock. Phoebe and Frank were killed in a crash two days later. The car caught fire and the intensity of the heat burnt the tarmac. Skye was the only survivor, untouched by the flames. No one knew how she got out alive. She went to live in Orford with her grandmother, Mrs Berry.

In the summer holidays I went to see Skye. Mrs Berry was very good with her. They seemed well suited, sitting quietly together in that pretty little cottage. Skye took me outside to show me the garden and I asked how she had survived the crash. She said after they'd locked away the nasty man they were chased by the people, the bad people, who looked after him. Then all went dark and lonely.

'It will be lonely until I can jump,' she said.

I tried to ask more questions but it was pointless. She put her fingers to her lips and said all would be well as long as they didn't turn on the light.

I gave up after that. I never went to see her again. I missed Phoebe too much.

Blame the stone, blame Skye, blame me.

REX MULLER

Chapter Seventeen

You've spoken to Mari? It's been terrible for her, the not knowing – it makes you lose your mind. Where was I? That's right – you have some memory, Mr Jones.

I was sixteen when I left home. There was a woman called Phoebe Berry – her mother lived in Orford. Phoebe taught painting at the Royal College of Art in London and she helped me get a place at the Slade. She helped Mari too – she went to Central.

I was so relieved to be living in a bedsit, away from my family. Mari's flat was quite close but we never met up. I think neither of us wanted to talk about the night we found the stones. I threw myself into my work and tried to forget about Suffolk. I had no desire to rake up the past.

It was about five years later that I received a note. It simply said, 'I am a friend of your brother Lazarus.' And was signed 'Icarus'. I remember thinking that no one is called Icarus.

He said that he happened to be in London and would I like to meet up. He knew the pub round the corner from my studio.

I'll never forget when I first saw Icarus. He was certainly handsome, but he had something else about him, something I couldn't put my finger on. An aura, perhaps.

We sat and had a beer. He said he liked the country better than London. He said he had been delighted to meet Lazarus.

I asked him why.

He didn't answer and I wondered what he was after and why he was there. We started talking, or rather, he talked. I listened and for the first time since Luke died I felt there was someone who was curious about loneliness, what it felt like to lose someone you loved, the emotional cost of irreplaceable love. I didn't want him to leave. I was fascinated by the way he looked and I asked him if he would sit for me. He wanted to know what that entailed. I said, standing very still, and he said he was good at that. He agreed to come the next day to my studio. Just as he was leaving he asked if I knew Lazarus had a girlfriend, Skye? I think I burst out laughing. I found it almost impossible to imagine Lazarus with a girl.

My studio then was in a disused factory by King's Cross, a hard place to get into. You went up some concrete stairs and then you had to know the code for the door. It was a rough area so I padlocked my studio door on the outside when I left it, and bolted it when I was inside. The other artists who had studios there called my place 'Fort Knox'.

I was getting set up when Icarus appeared. I just turned around and there he was. Dressed in an eighteenth-century waistcoat and jacket, he looked utterly extraordinary. I asked him how he'd got in. He shrugged and said something about someone letting him in, but I knew that was impossible. The artist in me refused to be daunted by the practical. He was beautifully dressed and stood just as I would have placed him.

He rang the bell next time he came. In all, I did six sessions with him. He asked me to paint him without his glasses and I took a great deal of care over his eyes. They were hypnotic, as dark as the universe. I never felt I did them justice.

I went up to Eyke with Icarus to see my brother and meet his girlfriend.

For the first time Mum and Dad seemed a little more normal. They had invited Skye for tea with her grandmother, Mrs Berry. I hadn't realised until then that Skye was Phoebe's adopted daughter. I'd heard, of course, about the car accident that had killed Phoebe and Frank. Mrs Berry seemed much taken with Icarus. As for my brother, it was the only time since his resurrection that I'd seen him being almost human. I had the feeling Mrs Berry understood Skye, unlike my parents, who seemed to have no connection at all with Lazarus.

It was an awkward weekend but I remember thinking Lazarus and Skye were made for one another, in a way I couldn't explain. I felt they had grown out of the same stone.

As I was leaving, Lazarus said, 'We have to go home.'

'You are home,' I said.

He shook his head and said, 'We must jump. We have to jump.'

I couldn't wait to leave. Only as the train left Ipswich for London did I feel calm once more. I had hoped to see Icarus again to show him the painting but I had no address for him, no phone number, no idea who he really was.

I heard on the news about Lazarus and Skye. I went home as if for a funeral, except there were no coffins, no bodies, no body parts, nothing to bury. I thought my parents would be heartbroken and instead I found they could barely remember who Lazarus was. They seemed happy, free, almost back to their old selves. They had stopped taking the medication. When I tried to talk to Mum about my brother, she looked surprised and said that Luke had died when he was eleven. They never mentioned Lazarus again.

It was then I knew how much I missed Luke, how much I longed to have him back.

That's all I want to say, Mr Jones.

JAZMIN LITTLE

Chapter Eighteen

I think it was the following day that Becky and me went to Mrs Berry's. Yes, it must've been the Thursday because on the Friday the removal lorry was coming. The key was left under a stone. Can't imagine doing that in London. It was a small cottage and had a lovely feel to it – you know, fireplace, rose and peony wallpaper, pictures of haystacks, that sort of thing. It was as neat as if Mrs Berry had just gone to the shops and would be back in a jiffy. Not as if she'd been bundled off to an old people's home to rot and be forgotten.

'What's she left you?' I asked Becky.

'Those,' she said, pointing to a collection of old-fashioned china ladies in full skirts, holding baskets and balloons.

'What're you going to do with them?' I asked.

'Keep them,' said Becky. 'I loved coming here when I was small. I used to ask Mrs Berry if I could live with her.'

'Why?'

'She made me feel safe.'

'I always thought that you had the ideal family,' I said.

Becky laughed. 'That's the trouble with the grass, Jaz. It's always greener in someone else's backyard. Just 'cause there's money, it doesn't mean there's happiness. Mrs Berry used to say, "These will be yours when I'm gone," but she isn't gone and all this stinks. She's been removed by uncaring, greedy relatives.'

There wasn't a lot to say to that. I looked around the cottage. Two bedrooms upstairs, bathroom next to the kitchen. I went into the garden. Mrs Berry had green fingers – grew roses and all her own veg. The last place she needed to be in was an old people's home. It seemed to me that she had a full set of marbles. I was thinking that she wouldn't live long if she couldn't come home to this, when I noticed a small, blacked-out, mesh-covered window, which I didn't remember seeing inside the cottage. I went back in but there definitely wasn't a room that lined up with the window. I looked again and was even more puzzled. Why, in such a small cottage, would you want to block off a room?

'Shall we go?' said Becky. She'd found a cardboard box and some newspaper for the china ladies.

'Come and look at this,' I said.

We went into the garden and I pointed out the window.

'It looks as if it comes off the kitchen,' said Becky, going back in. 'It must be behind this dresser.'

The dresser was jammed full of china and all sorts of stuff.

I looked at Becky. Becky looked at me.

'All right,' she said. 'Let's do it.'

It took a good hour to take off all the breakables and to budge the thing out of the way. We were rewarded with the sight of a door covered in cobwebs and dust. My heart started to dance the fandango. Don't know why – intuition, maybe.

Becky tried to open it but it was taped and painted shut. We both pushed and finally it gave way and we tumbled into a pantry. Before us stood a waxwork of a young man, illuminated by the morning sun. His face was white, his eyes closed, he had a piercing through his nose and small numbers tattooed in a band around his forehead, his hair shaved into a Mohican. He was wearing a leather-studded jacket and a torn T-shirt held together with safety pins. His arms were too long. His feet were bare.

'That's weird,' said Becky. 'Why would anyone wall up a waxwork dummy?'

'It gives me the creeps,' I said.

That's when I saw the waxwork's big toe move.

'Oh, shit! Oh, holy shit!' said Becky.

His eyes opened and stared straight at us. They weren't human, Mr Jones. His irises had no colour.

I don't think I've ever moved so fast. We slammed the pantry door shut and were trying to push the dresser back when the pantry door exploded. Shards of wood rained down. We cowered behind the dresser in terror. The dummy backed into the kitchen, arms outstretched, bathing, or so it appeared, in the sunlight.

Mr Jones, I know you're being polite, listening to all this crap and most probably thinking what a load of cobblers. Everyone else has said so. What would make you different? It doesn't matter how many times I tell it, I've never been believed.

You do? Well, you're one in a million, Mr Jones. Does it make any sense, the idea of a dummy coming to life? But we haven't got to the part that gives me nightmares, that makes me sleep with the lights on. I was accused of fabrication, but I don't think I have the imagination to make up this stuff.

It was the back of his head that made me ache with fear, that made lolly sticks of my legs. It was transparent; you could see through his skull to the wires in his brain. It sounds crazy, but it looked like he was half flesh, half something else. When he moved, lights flickered on and off in his head. We weren't breathing when he turned to face us. I remember thinking: oh no, oh no, we've really had it. We've really, really had it. And this is no clockwork dummy.

His eyes now had colour to them. They were red. He walked towards us, he grinned, stuck out his tongue and licked his dry lips.

Becky swallowed a scream as he put his finger on her forehead.

'You speak. You speak my message. Say, he should never have abandoned me. Tell Icarus – I will find him, kill him.'

Becky was shaking. Then, in a blur of speed, he vanished.

There was a bright red mark on her forehead where his finger had been.

'What have we done?' I said. 'Let's get out of here.'

'Jaz,' said Becky. 'Wait. Look what's in the pantry.'

The light from the kitchen shone directly onto the back wall, where hung a portrait in a simple frame. It glimmered like a jewel. It was the kind of thing you would see in an art gallery, not

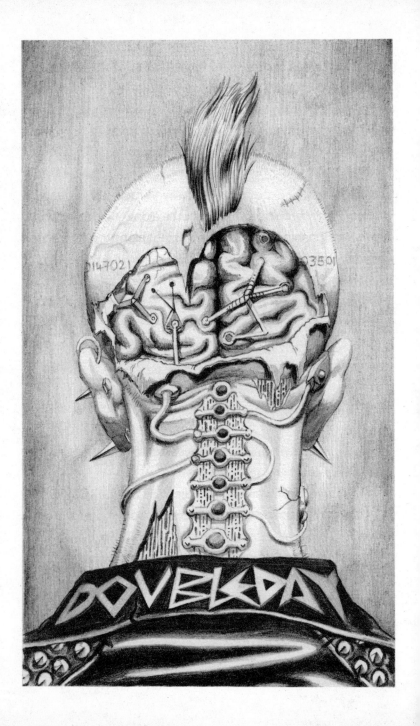

hidden away in a blacked-out room. There was no question of who it was. Icarus, a life-sized head.

We stopped dead. Someone was knocking on the front door. We sank onto the floor.

'Hallo, dears, it's me,' came the unmistakable voice of Mrs Sunshine.

You know that expression – between a rock and . . . death?

We froze, watching a mouse scuttle along the skirting board while Mrs Sunshine kept knocking. I crept along the floor to the back door and locked it just in time, for there she was again.

'Becky,' called Mrs Sunshine. 'Are you there, dear?'

By the time she'd finally taken her nose out of the keyhole, it felt like we had crouched there for a whole day.

Becky hurriedly wrapped up her figurines and put them in a cardboard box.

'Hold this,' she said.

'Why?' I said, taking it like a muppet as she slipped back into the pantry.

'We can't leave this behind,' she said, bringing out the portrait and putting it in the box.

We closed the front door as quietly as we could and Becky posted the keys back through the letterbox. We heard them thud onto the mat.

We found Mrs Sunshine waiting for us by the garden gate. She had on gardening gloves and held a pair of secateurs. She reminded me of a crab.

'Oh, Becky,' she said. 'Good. You've taken what you wanted? Left the keys under the stone?'

'Oh dear,' said Becky, sounding artificially bright. 'I completely forgot. I posted them through the letterbox. Is that a problem?'

You could see by the lightning flash of annoyance that crossed Mrs Sunshine's face that she was miffed. I watched, fascinated, as she made a visible effort to muster all her features into a regiment of a smile.

'Never mind, dear. It must have been all the sadness,' she said. 'I'll have to collect the spare set from Mrs Morris.' She made it sound as if she would have to dig a tunnel to Outer Mongolia via Birmingham to collect them.

She turned to me and pointed across the street. 'The house on the corner. That's where I live.' She said it as if it explained everything. In the front garden was a hedge made out of a tortured tree. I could see all the plants were living under the martial law of Mrs Sunshine's secateurs.

Becky and me were doing our level best to look as if we were characters in a Jane Austen novel. Though, come to think about it, I can't remember there being that many girls like me in her books.

Mrs Sunshine started to talk about Mrs Berry and how terrible it was that her relatives had gone back to Australia. On and on she went. How was Ruth? How was Simon? By the glint in her eye I had a feeling that the bad news had spread through the village faster than a flying kipper. She stared at Becky's forehead.

'You have a red mark, did you know?' said Mrs Sunshine. 'Is it paint?'

'Yes,' said Becky. 'Goodbye.'

'Well, of course. I'd better be bobbing along if I'm ever going to retrieve those keys.'

Yes, I thought, and double yes.

When we got home, the first thing we did was go round the whole house and check that every door, every window, was locked, making sure old red-eyes hadn't broken into the house. Though seeing what he could do to doors, I doubted he would have much of a problem with ours.

'You don't think we just imagined all that? I mean, think about it. It couldn't have happened, could it?' said Becky.

'Not unless we were on drugs, and we weren't. Sorry, Becky, but he seemed pretty solid to me.'

'I've got a terrible headache,' she said as she propped up the painting on the kitchen table.

'He looks like someone out of a Georgette Heyer novel,' I said. 'I wonder who painted it.'

'The minute Mrs Sunshine gets into the cottage,' said Becky, 'she'll think we did all that, and then what?'

'All hell and all bells will break loose,' I said. 'We'll have to tell the truth.'

'You're joking. Who will believe us?' She went to look in the mirror. 'What is this?' She tried to rub off the red mark on her forehead.

'Jaz,' she said, her voice panicky. 'It won't come off.'

Chapter Nineteen

I like a good story, Mr Jones, but I like it when things make sense, and that dummy becoming live didn't make any sense.

Once Becky had calmed down about the red mark on her forehead and had a cup of tea she said, 'Hungry?'

'I don't think I could eat a thing,' I said. 'My stomach has gone to glue.'

'Even with a headache I'm famished,' said Becky and she took out a jar of peanut butter and started to eat it by the spoonful.

Becky eating.

She ate, staring at the painting, trying to be Sherlock and not succeeding. Finally, Becky pushed the jar aside and picked up the phone.

'Who are you calling?'

'The Beeches Retirement Home,' she said. 'I want to go and see Mrs Berry.'

'Wait,' I said. 'Wait, we should think this through.'

But as usual Becky had gone right ahead. There was no reverse gear to any of her actions. The deed was already done.

'Hello,' said Becky. 'Yeah, I wonder if you could tell me what time visiting hours are? Oh, I see ... Mrs Berry. My name is Becky Burns. Will you tell her I'll be there this afternoon?' She hung up and turned to me. 'You up for this?'

'You want me to come?'

'Of course. She's the only person who might be able to explain that thing in the pantry.'

'What if that thing, as you call it, comes back?'

Becky didn't answer and dialled the minicab number.

Nothing happens fast in the country. London time didn't register at that distance from the city. We waited an hour before the minicab arrived. The driver, a woman, had nothing to say. Dull worked well for me.

The retirement home was up a gravel drive, a large red-brick gothic house with a conservatory sticking out of one side. It was there in the goldfish bowl we found Mrs Berry sitting in an ugly chair. Why do old people have to live out their last days in such hideous chairs? She was heaped into it, staring out the window at a dull, green, endless lawn where a rambling rose would never dare to stray.

She appeared to be made of bread dough, more flesh than bone – she sort of spread into her cardigan. She was wearing slippers with pom-poms on them. That was about the only cheery thing that afternoon, the word pom-pom.

Mrs Berry's face burst into a cherry-pie smile when she saw Becky.

'Have you come to take me home?' she said. 'Good girl. I'll just get my hat and scarf.' Making no effort to move from the chair, she dropped her voice. 'I don't like it here.'

'Tea, Edith?' said a carer. 'And some of that coffee cake you like?'

Mrs Berry nodded. 'Shop-bought,' she whispered to us. 'Do you remember my coffee cake, Rebecca?'

'Yes,' said Becky. 'It was special. And you'd let me lick the bowl.'

'You always said that was the best bit.' She waved in the direction of the carer. 'I don't like her calling me Edith. You would think I'm on her Christmas card list.'

'They don't mean any harm by it,' said Becky, but Mrs Berry had gone back to staring out of the window at the rain that was now trickling down the glass pane in front of her.

'When I was little,' she said, 'me and my sister would put bets on which raindrop would arrive at the bottom of the window first.'

I was beginning to think I'd made a mistake and Mrs Berry hadn't the full set of marbles after all. Becky found two footstools and we sat either side of her.

Becky took her hand and said, 'We went to your cottage today.'

Mrs Berry seemed not to hear. 'He promised he wouldn't leave me here,' she said. 'He told me I had to be patient and he would know when he was needed. I want to go home, now that he hasn't come as he promised.'

'Who promised? Your nephew?' said Becky.

'No, not him.'

'Then who is it you're waiting for?'

'That would be telling, dear,' said Mrs Berry. 'And I said

nothing would pass my lips. I don't have a loose tongue and I don't feed off gossip, either.'

The carer returned with a china teapot and mismatched cups and saucers that would have looked cool anywhere but there.

'My daughter wouldn't have let this happen,' said Mrs Berry. 'Phoebe would have had it out with that nephew of mine. I don't belong here. I want to go home.'

'Where is she?' I asked. 'Your daughter.'

Becky gave me a look that made it quite clear I hadn't asked the right question.

'She was such a lovely girl, my Phoebe – a lot like you, Rebecca.' She patted Becky's hand. 'You always reminded me of her – the same curious expression. She never could leave a stone alone. No, that's not right . . . I mean upended. Never leave a stone upended.'

Becky said, 'We found the pantry.'

Mrs Berry's face lost its smile.

'You shouldn't have done that. No one should go in there.'

'Why not?'

'Because of the man with the red eyes. His mind's all twisted, wired wrong. Now you've let him out, he'll find him, kill him.'

So, I thought. Not so many screws missing from this self-assembly bookcase.

'I don't understand,' said Becky.

'You are to have the Doulton figurines,' said Mrs Berry. 'I told you they'd be yours when I'm gone.'

'You're not gone,' said Becky.

'I will be soon. He will come for me. I haven't given up believing.' She gazed out of the window again. 'He said he would.'

'Do you mean Jesus?' asked Becky and then, seeing that Mrs Berry was not going to answer, she changed the subject. 'Who painted the portrait?'

Mrs Berry took a bite of cake and crumbs fell onto her cardigan. 'That monster will find him, he blames him.'

'Blames who?'

Silence.

Becky tried again. 'The painting,' she said. 'Who was the artist?'

'It was the last thing my daughter ever painted,' said Mrs Berry. 'Phoebe thought we would trick him.'

'Who?' said Becky. 'Trick who?'

'She said that it would explain everything, it would be her witness. Now, be a good girl, Rebecca, find my coat and my handbag and take me home.'

I stood, longing to be out of there. Mrs Berry turned and looked up at me.

'You didn't say your name, dear,' she said.

'Jazmin. Jazmin Little.'

'You're a beauty,' she said. 'Lovely eyes – dark and alive. Gems, your eyes are. Not like the man in the pantry. He walks wrong, looks wrong. No shoes. Red eyes. He shouldn't be here.' Her voice became loud and querulous. 'You should never have let the sunlight in.'

The carer came and bent over her.

'Edith, would you like to go back to your room?'

'No,' said Mrs Berry. 'I want to go home.'

'It happens,' said the carer to us. 'It can take a little time for some of our guests to settle in. Early days, isn't it, Edith?'

It was still raining when we went outside, and I tipped my head to the sky and took gulps of breath. May I not end my days in a cardigan and a dreadful chair eating shop-bought coffee cake.

'Let's go,' said Becky.

She let the rain run down her face but I could see she was crying.

'You all right?' I said. Goodness knows why, as it was as obvious as the red spot on her forehead that Becky was far from all right.

'I feel weird,' she said.

'Since when?' I asked. 'Since we arrived here? This place would suck the life out of the living. No wonder you feel odd.'

'No, since this red mark.'

It wasn't far to walk to Shingle Street. I'd never been there before. It was a long, stony beach with a row of houses on it. I really liked it and I remember thinking I wouldn't mind living there, until Becky told me about the locals who had set the sea on fire when the Germans tried to invade in the Second World War.

'That night, fishermen saw ghosts walking along the shore,' she added.

'Great,' I said. 'There goes another dream.'

'I want to show you something,' Becky said.

She took a white stone from her pocket and handed it to me. It was soft and radiated a gentle heat.

'Where did you get that from? A joke shop?'

'Icarus gave it to me when I saw him in prison. Look – it can do this.'

She threw it in the air and for a moment it disappeared then reappeared and she caught it.

That stone worried me. Alex had talked about white stones dropping from the alien craft in Rendlesham Forest.

So many things worried me. Becky's voracious appetite, for starters. No one gets cured from anorexia that easily. No one. My sister Kylie took years to recover from bulimia and still, if things went wrong, it would kick off again. Here was Becky, eating better than me, as if she'd never had a problem with food. Every mealtime I'd wait for her to go back to the not-eating game. How could one meeting with Icarus have cured her of anorexia?

The rain stopped and a watery sun broke through the clouds. We watched the waves hitting the pebbles, not wanting time to take us prisoner as it had Mrs Berry.

'What happened to Phoebe?' I asked.

Becky had a distant look in her eyes.

'She and her husband were killed in car crash. Their car burst into flames – burnt up the tarmac. It was so ferocious it left a crater in the road.'

Everything we talked about on that stony beach ended in death. I changed the subject.

'So – what's going on with you and Icarus?' I asked.

'What do you think of him?'

'I think maybe he's not of our world,' I said. 'I don't know. But you didn't answer my question.'

Becky stared at the white stone. 'I love him,' she said.

'Wait, Becky, no. This is crazy. Think of what Mrs Berry just said about the creep in the pantry. You don't need to be Sherlock bloody Holmes to work out he is after Icarus. And if – and I can't believe I'm even thinking this – if Icarus is an alien, the last thing you need is to get muddled up in all that shit. All right, he's helped you to eat again. Leave it there and –'

Becky interrupted my alien rap.

'Why don't you ever listen to me?'

'I do!'

'No, you don't. You're like all the rest. A smile, a pat on the back, let's talk about something else. Poor Becky this, poor Becky that. I've told you I love Icarus – he's the one. The *numero uno*, the main squeeze, whatever you wish to call him, and all you can say is "no" because he is an alien.' Her voice became louder with every furious word. 'Are you my friend or not? Those notebooks that he gave me, that no one has been able to decipher – they don't need a code. The minute I saw his writing I could read it, and he knew it. It's because he loves me that the words make sense. It's because I love him that I can read them.'

I'd never seen her this angry, not even when Simon told her he had left Ruth.

'Sorry,' was all I could say, and like all sorrys, the word failed to work.

Chapter Twenty

Before we'd left The Beeches, Becky had called for a minicab to pick us up from Shingle Street. I was glad to see it was the woman driver again.

Becky wasn't speaking to me.

We were nearing Orford when my phone bleeped.

where are you

are you all right

The texts were from Alex. I smiled. Silly how two messages from someone you fancy can make you feel ten feet tall. I noticed they'd been sent at three o'clock and then again at three-fifteen. It was now nearly seven. They'd taken four hours to come through. It was like being in the Dark Ages up there, and talking on tin cans. I should have known then that something was wrong. Alex wasn't the kind of person who sent the same message twice by accident. I quickly texted back, saying we were nearly home. He didn't reply.

I'd been thinking I might tell Becky about Alex and me but decided it was too soon and best to leave it. I felt rather awkward and anyway it didn't strike me that it was the day for that kind of conversation. It also might drag up the subject of Icarus again and that was a topic that could throw our friendship into the abyss for all eternity.

When Orford came into view we could see a plume of smoke rising above it.

'What's that?' I said.

'Perhaps it's the smoke house,' said Becky, not sounding convinced.

By the time we'd reached Pump Street the air stank of acrid smoke – unlike the high-class, perfumed, wood-burning-stove smoke that usually wafted around the village.

I spotted Alex outside the bakery. My heart soared when I saw him – and plummeted when he started speaking.

'Where have you been?' he said, his tone cold.

Becky explained that we had been to see Mrs Berry.

'You were going to her cottage today,' he said. It was a statement of fact rather than anything to be disputed.

'Yes,' said Becky. 'We went, and I picked up the Doulton figurines she left for me.'

'You didn't light anything in the cottage?' Alex said.

'No – why would I?'

'You didn't turn on the cooker, have a fag, light a candle?'

'No,' said Becky. This time she didn't sound quite so certain. 'What's happened?'

Alex's face softened.

'I came here on my moped the minute I heard.'

'Heard what?' asked Becky.

'About the fire at Mrs Berry's cottage. It was on the local news.'

I felt a chill run down my spine.

'I was worried you might have gone to the cottage this afternoon,' said Alex. 'So I went straight there. I spoke to the fire officer – he said it went up as fast as kindling. If anyone had been inside they wouldn't have stood a chance. Why do you never answer your phone?'

'How did it catch fire?' I asked, though I wanted to ask where the fire had started, for I had a terrible feeling that I knew the answer to that one.

'They don't know yet, but the fire officer thought it started in the pantry. I didn't know there was a pantry. I never saw one in all the time I went there, did you, Becks?'

'No,' said Becky. It was that 'no' that became the lock on the door of a lie.

One lie, two lies, three lies and all truth lies ripped apart. But once Becky had said that 'no' and said it so firmly, there was nothing to do but go along with it.

We walked to where the two fire engines were parked, plus police cars and a rescue unit. All the inhabitants of Orford seemed to have gathered to stare at the charred remains of Mrs Berry's cottage.

We went into the Burnses' house through the back door. I was glad we'd had the nous to hide the painting before we'd headed off for the retirement home.

'Tea,' I said, and filled the kettle while Alex examined the china figurines.

I thought, that's what all British people do when they don't understand what's going on: make a nice cup of tea. I tell you,

Mr Jones, when the end of the world comes, Britain will whistle to the sound of all those kettles on the boil.

The doorbell rang; Becky went to answer it. I could hear voices in the hall and then two police officers came in.

One was a woman who looked at me and said, 'Are you Jazmin Little?'

I nodded. Never been that keen on the police – where I come from they mean trouble, either for you or someone you know.

'I want to ask you both questions about the fire in Mrs Berry's cottage this afternoon. You were the last people to be seen there.'

Mrs Sunshine hadn't wasted a moment in doing her civic duty. Becky did the talking; I just nodded. When asked if we'd gone into the pantry, I couldn't think why we didn't just tell the truth. But I suppose if we had done we would have had to hand over the painting. I knew that Becky had no intention of doing that.

By the time the two officers left it was getting dark and I was starving. I started to make supper. I wanted Alex to stay, wanted to have a chance to talk to him alone. But that evening it proved impossible because suddenly Becky went from not talking to me to talking so much affectionate dribble about me that I was embarrassed. I felt it was coded language for 'Don't say a word, Jaz, about the pantry or the painting. Don't say a word.'

I was wondering if Alex had gone off me because he hardly looked in my direction. At ten he stood up and said he should be going.

'Stay,' said Becky. 'We can watch a film. I'll make popcorn.'

To my surprise he agreed. Horror films are not really up

my street. This one was about seven teenagers who spend a weekend in a spooky old house. All but one ends up dead. Becky's popcorn was good though.

We went to bed about twelve-thirty. Becky was staying in the main bedroom that had this enormous four-poster bed. Six people could sleep in it comfortably.

I went in to ask how she was feeling. She said she still felt a little weird.

'This red spot really throbs.' I was by the door when she sat up. 'Oh, I left my rucksack downstairs.'

'You stay in bed,' I said. And I ran down to get it for her.

I had my own bedroom with a big double bed. Alex usually slept in the guest room but he didn't stay there for long that night because he came to see me. All I will say is that I was wrong. He hadn't gone off me. I don't know what time we fell asleep but I know it was three o'clock when we woke to the sound of Becky screaming. Alex took a towelling dressing gown with huge daisies on it from the back of the door. I pulled on the dress I'd been wearing the day before and we ran downstairs. Becky was in the kitchen with a glass of water in her hand.

'He's out there,' she said, pointing to the picture windows.

'Who?' said Alex, as he found a torch. He had his hand on the door handle, ready to go outside.

'No!' we both screamed.

'It isn't safe,' said Becky. 'He's dangerous.'

'I can't see anyone,' said Alex. 'It's that film we watched – it's given you the freaks.'

I was nearly down on the cinema floor with the popcorn, I was so damned scared at that moment. Alex turned on all the kitchen lights and the security lights in the garden came on automatically.

'What did he look like?'

'A punk with a Mohican haircut,' said Becky. 'He had red eyes and no shoes,' she added.

'That's a bit prehistoric,' said Alex.

The mark on Becky's forehead had begun to bleed.

'What the fuck is going on?' I said.

Becky was shaking.

'Calm down, both of you. Here, Becky,' he handed her a tissue. 'It's only a zit that's burst.'

'I don't know how much more of this weird shit I can take,' I said.

'What weird shit?' asked Alex.

'It's nothing,' said Becky, 'but perhaps we should all stay together.'

I definitely felt that was a good idea.

'I'm going to call the police,' Alex said. He picked up the house phone, then put it down again.

'What is it?' I said.

'It's dead.' He tried his mobile without any success. 'OK,' said Alex. He sounded a little less confident than he had a moment before. 'We'll stay together and deal with it in the morning.'

We all went upstairs to Becky's bedroom. We didn't turn off the lights. We did draw the blinds. We lay there listening to our hearts beating, an owl hooting, and that's when we heard the kitchen door being rattled.

'It's just the wind,' said Alex.

After what we had seen in Mrs Berry's cottage, I wasn't that convinced.

'Breathe, both of you,' said Alex when all was quiet again. 'It's only . . .' Alex didn't finish what he was saying because we could hear someone or something coming slowly up the stairs.

Becky had grabbed her mobile and was desperately tapping. 'Why doesn't this sodding thing work?'

Outside in the hall someone walked up and down. Then tried the door knob. Then there was silence again. Then a fist smashed through the wood panelling of the bedroom door.

'What the fuck!' shouted Alex.

I think we screamed. Maybe we didn't. To tell you the truth, I can't remember. The next thing I was conscious of, it was eleven o'clock in the morning. I never slept that long – usually I was up much earlier. Something to do with the birds and the bees and that blooming cockerel across the way. But it was a battle to stay awake – all of me longed for sleep. Alex was out cold. Becky was lying there with her eyes wide open, staring at the remains of the bedroom door.

'I'd hoped it was a nightmare,' she said.

I told her I would make us some tea and climbed out of bed.

I didn't recognise the kitchen. Everything had been trashed, or rather, everything had been methodically taken to pieces: all the kitchen units were unscrewed from the walls, all the cupboards emptied. It was a combination of a building site and a high-class junkyard. All I could think was that the noise involved in such destruction would surely have woken us. I do remember a sound that seemed to come from me.

Alex told me later that I'd hit my head on the table because I had fallen unconscious to the floor. I gave myself a nasty bruise. It was only when the police arrived shortly afterwards that we realised we'd slept all through Friday and Saturday and it was now Sunday morning.

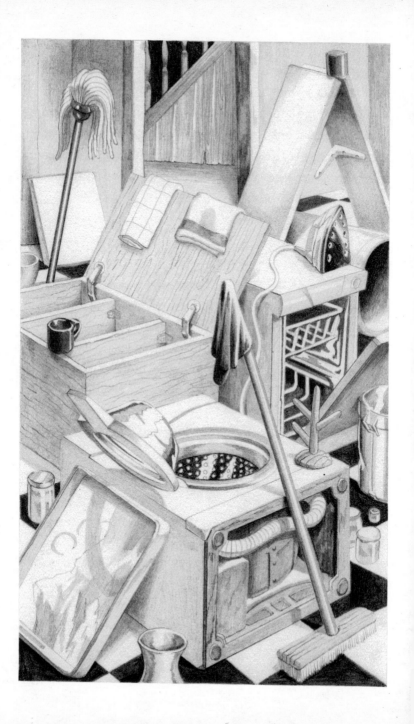

Chapter Twenty-One

The woman police officer who had questioned us on Thursday turned up again that morning. She was becoming an unpleasant habit that I wished we could break. She said her name was Fisher. She said she'd told me that before. With her came a detective who was called August. At least, I thought that was what he said. My brain was so juggled that names became pictures, and I remember thinking that August was a time for fishing.

Sergeant Fisher wanted to know if we'd taken any drugs. She really had a wasps' nest in her bonnet about that.

'Any mind-altering substances?' she asked for the twentieth time.

I couldn't see what was wrong with the answer 'no'. No was the truth.

The detective weighed up Alex and then said he had known cases where even a skinny lad like Alex could cause a great deal of destruction if he'd taken LSD.

'Why would I want to dismantle my father's house?' said Alex.

I don't know why I became spokesperson but I did.

'No,' I said again. 'All we took was popcorn. We watched a film and had popcorn.'

Detective August wasn't the sunniest of men. January might have suited him better.

The detective flicked through his notes.

'You are Alexander Burns?' he said.

'Yep. Becky is my sister. Half-sister, if you want to be accurate. Personally, I hate splitting the difference.'

Becky was clinging onto her orange rucksack as people cling onto lifebuoys when shipwrecked. She was the sleepiest of us all.

A doctor arrived to examine us. Then a procession of people in white boiler suits and blue plastic gloves went into the kitchen. I really wish I could remember the order all this happened in, Mr Jones, but that morning was a complete daze.

Nothing made much sense until Mari turned up in a sail of colourful fabric, her hair tied in a scarf, and the sight of her made me feel that everything might be all right. The morning would become the afternoon and the day would anchor itself in Sunday. I'd always had this crazy idea of the perfect mum, one who would be there to make you tea after school, worry about your teeth, that sort of thing. And the minute I saw Mari I thought, this is the woman I would have loved for a mum.

She looked relieved to see her son. He stood and she gave him a hug.

'I thought you were on the boat.' Then to me she said, 'You must be Jazmin.' And she put out her hand to me. 'Alex has told me about you.'

I came over all shy, as if I was in the school playground and the secret of the first kiss was all over my face, as if she knew about Alex and me. She saw Becky, staring at nothing, and knelt down beside her.

'Becky, it's Mari,' she said. 'Remember me?'

Becky nodded.

Mari spoke to the doctor.

'Becky isn't well,' she said. 'I'll take her home with me.'

But the doctor insisted that he had to do blood tests, and that they had to be done at the police station. We went in Mari's car. We kept falling asleep and the time in the police station was punctuated by plastic cups of coffee. Becky wouldn't let go of the orange rucksack. When the detective asked to see what was inside, Becky woke up.

'No. Leave it alone,' she said. 'It's private – it's my work.'

I could see the detective thought that it was her drug stash.

Finally she handed it over and then I realised why she had been clinging to it. Out came her computer, Icarus's exercise book, the magic-shop stone, and, wrapped in Mrs Berry's tea cloth, the painting.

Detective August flicked through the exercise book but, amazingly, didn't seem to have much interest in art. Something in Mari's face told me she had seen the painting before.

'Becky Burns – of course, you're the writer,' he said, as Becky put everything back. '*The Martian Winter*.' A smile nearly formed on his face but at the last minute he had a change of heart.

Mari took us to her home in her beaten-up old Volvo. It

smelled of dog. I remember thinking what a comforting smell it was, though I'd never had a dog. She lived not far from the River Dedham in a barn that had been converted into a house. It was the kind of place you see in magazines described with words like 'shabby chic'. No minimalism there, it was full of bosomy sofas, lots of books, paintings and sculptures. I didn't know that Alex had twin brothers – Jake and Ben. They were about nine and just asked question after question – not about what had happened to their brother but about the police station and what the detective looked like. I felt really at home and thought, forget Shingle Street, this is my manor.

Becky had hardly said a word.

I sat with her and said, 'Talk to me, Becks.'

She looked at me as if I was a stranger, then said, 'Icarus is in danger.' I was glad that Mari was in the kitchen and hadn't heard her. 'The man with the red eyes wants to destroy him, I'm certain of that. Jaz, we did a terrible thing,' she whispered. 'We should never have gone in the pantry. We should never have let him out.'

At that moment, the door opened and a Labrador ran in, followed by Mari's husband, Tom, laden with fishing tackle.

'Alex,' he said. 'Are you OK, son?'

'Yeah, I'm fine, Dad,' Alex replied, and you could see by the way he looked at his stepfather that he meant every one of those three letters.

'You're Jazmin,' said Tom to me, with a warm smile.

Becky hardly noticed when Tom greeted her. 'I have to talk to him,' she said.

'Who?' said Mari, coming in with the tea.

'Icarus,' said Becky.

Mari went pale and I thought she was going to drop the tray. I went to help her.

'That's a name from the past,' said Tom. 'No one can see Icarus, Becky, love. He's still in prison.'

We had tea. Becky played with a slice of fruit cake.

'Eat up, Becks,' said Alex. He was sitting next to me on the sofa.

'I can't,' she said. 'I keep hearing this voice in my head and it won't go away.'

'What does it say, this voice of yours?' asked Tom.

Becky didn't reply. She closed her eyes and then I nearly jumped out of my skin. For a nightmare of a moment I thought the red-eyed man was in the house, but the voice was coming from Becky, thick with the sound of cobwebs. Her breath was short, her eyes tight closed.

'Tell Icarus I have risen – and I will kill him.'

Jake and Ben stared at her in wonder; I stared at her in horror. The spot on her forehead had started to bleed again. Alex reached for my hand.

To my surprise, Mari said, 'Who are you?'

'I am Doubleday,' said the voice.

Chapter Twenty-Two

'Are you going to speak funny again?' asked Jake.

The twins were eating their cereal when Becky came down, still clutching her rucksack. Ben imitated the voice they'd heard last night and Becky stared at them as if they were Martians.

'Come on, you two monkeys, eat up,' said Tom, and before they could say another word, 'The car, now, or you'll be late for your sailing lesson.'

They stampeded out of the house and the door slammed behind them.

I was more than pleased to see them go. Last night, Mari and Tom had done their best to make light of Becky's behaviour for the boys' sake, though there was nothing light about it.

'How are you feeling?' asked Mari, examining Becky's forehead. The spot had vanished.

'Fine,' said Becky.

'Fine' is an awful word. It didn't describe Becky and it didn't describe how we were all feeling.

Mari sat with us at the kitchen table.

'Something is going on, Alex,' she said. 'Tell me, for goodness' sake. Tell me, I won't be cross.'

One lie, two lies, and all truth lies shattered.

'Are you keeping something important from me?'

I felt like shouting, 'Yes, yes – there's a hell of a lot more to all this. The trouble is, no one is ever going to believe us.'

But Alex took a different tack. 'You've seen that painting before, haven't you, Mum?'

'Yes,' said Mari. 'Yes, a long time ago, in Phoebe Berry's flat in London. I asked her who the subject was and how she knew him. I found out later that she'd met Icarus wandering on the beach at Shingle Street. Becky – where did you find the painting?'

I longed for Becky to speak, to finally mouth the truth. I felt if anyone was likely to understand all the strangeness it would be Mari. I could see Becky struggling with the idea. Just as she got to the first word, the doorbell rang. What do comedians tell you about timing? But this was no comedy, it couldn't be, the timing was all wrong. I thought it must be Sergeant Fisher and was bracing myself for another onslaught of questions when an unexpected hurricane blew in. Simon and Tess.

Tess glanced round the house with a glint of approval, then, ignoring Mari, went to Becky.

'Oh my God, Becky, darling, how terrible!' she said. 'Are you all right? It must've been so frightening.'

Simon couldn't ignore Mari and smiled at her sheepishly.

'We came as soon as we could,' he said. Mari said nothing. Which didn't deter Simon one little bit. Someone had to talk;

silence was not appropriate. Nobly, Simon took on the task. 'I spoke to Detective August this morning. He said it wasn't a regular sort of robbery.'

'It wasn't a robbery.' Me and my big mouth could be up there for the Oscars. Simon took no notice.

'He also told me that he believes that you all know more than you let on.'

Simon was just getting into his stride, about to gear up to righteous indignation. When I was small I thought righteous indignation was an indigestion tablet. Funny how often a child gets something right even when it's wrong.

'We drove straight up here,' interrupted Tess. 'I couldn't believe what the police said, the kitchen trashed.'

Tess's main concern was that Becky should go back to London right away; there was no question of her staying in Orford on her own.

'She's not on her own,' said Simon. 'She has Jazmin.'

Tess chose to ignore this fact.

In all the argy-bargy the wishes of Becky herself seemed to have been forgotten. Simon put his arm around her and she stiffened.

'I don't want to go to London,' she said.

Her father looked relieved. 'I think,' he said, 'if you're happy to stay up here with Jazmin –' he turned to me as if the two thousand pounds had bought him an ally for life – 'then maybe it's for the best. I've spoken to a builder and he said that he would look in and see the damage for himself. I'm having a better alarm system fitted,' he added, as if that would guarantee our safety.

You morons, I wanted to shout at him and Tess. Both of you are complete basket cases. Of course Becky shouldn't return to the house.

'Mari,' said Simon, 'you'll keep an eye on them?'

That he hadn't mentioned Alex should have been a sign of what was about to come. I'd noticed when I'd lived with the Burnses that Simon worked on the principle that someone was always to blame. The vortex of the storm was about to surround Alex.

'Simon, I think Becky should stay here with Mum and Tom,' Alex said. 'She saw someone in the garden last night.'

Simon, who I'd never seen angry before, turned a greyish blue. Only his nose remained red.

'I wasn't going to mention it,' he said. Now he was going to mention it. 'Detective August thinks that the intruder Becky thought she saw was a hallucination brought on by taking an illegal substance, and that it was you who dismantled the kitchen units. He doesn't believe that anyone else was involved. There were no fingerprints or footprints other than yours and Becky's and Jazmin's. The girls wouldn't have had the strength to cause so much destruction. So that leaves you. Frankly, Alex, I feel you should contribute to the cost of rebuilding the kitchen.'

I said, a little too quickly, 'Alex hasn't done anything wrong.'

'Did you supply the girls with drugs, Alex?' continued Simon.

'No, he didn't,' I said. 'We ate popcorn. Popcorn is not an illegal substance.'

Alex was furious. 'I don't do drugs, Simon.'

Tess turned to me. 'Then was it you who supplied the drugs?'

I should have seen that coming. Why not blame the girl from the council estate?

Simon ignored Tess. 'I want all of you to tidy up the house before the builders arrive. I don't want any excuses from any of you, especially not you, Alex, who I hold totally responsible for all that has happened.'

Mari had had enough. 'Why do you always think everything is Alex's fault? You blame him when anything goes wrong. He is eighteen years old and very responsible. You've been no sort of father to him and you have no right to come barging in here, accusing him of taking drugs. You have no evidence and neither does that blinkered detective.'

Go Mari, go girl, I thought. She was building up for a major argument and I could see Simon wanted to avoid having a major argument in front of Tess. By the look on Tess's face, I think it was just dawning on her that Simon had married, had a child with and left two women, and it was likely she was going to be the next in line. Or as Becky had said, with a terrible French accent, 'the turd wife'. That had made me laugh.

Having won the pathetic argument, Simon and Tess spiralled out of our lives, leaving Alex completely flattened.

'He's a shit,' he said. 'He always thinks the worst of me.'

Mari said, 'And he's always wrong, love. He may be your biological father but he's not the one you call Dad.'

'Yeah, I know,' said Alex. 'But still, it bugs me.'

Chapter Twenty-Three

Mari gave us lunch and said she would come and help us clean up the house. I tell you, that seemed like the best idea we'd heard all morning. We needed someone to be with us, that was for shizzle.

Ziggy the dog looked fed up to be left behind but it turned out to be a good thing we didn't take him. I don't remember that we said a lot on the journey back to Orford. We were all lost in our own thoughts. It was just as we neared the village that Mari's mobile rang. It was Tom to say he'd had to leave work to go to Ipswich Hospital – there'd been an accident during the sailing class. Jake had broken his leg and needed an operation.

'I have to go,' Mari said. 'I'm sorry, will you be all right?'

'Yes,' said Alex. 'You sure you don't want me to come with you, Mum?'

I often wonder what would have happened if she had said yes. You don't always see paths clearly, but that was another path, the path not taken. If only he had gone, what then?

Mari said, 'No, stay with the girls. I'll call you this evening to see how you're doing.'

I watched her reverse the car and drive away. I had this sinking feeling that with her all hope of this ending well was fast disappearing in exhaust fumes.

As we arrived at the house, Alex noticed a car outside.

'You don't see many of those Ford Orions,' he said.

I don't care much for cars. As long as they move, don't break down, have enough seats, that's good enough for me.

Becky only glanced at it.

The minute we entered the house, we knew something was wrong. The place was eerily spick and span. As for the kitchen, it was as if nothing had happened, apart from two of the cabinet doors that were hanging off their hinges.

'I don't like this,' said Becky. 'I don't like this one little . . .'

I've never been that keen on clichés, and Becky didn't manage to finish hers because we could see through the hall into the lounge, where stood two men. They both wore suits in varying degrees of dark. They both wore mirrored sunglasses. They didn't look like the police; I know what the police look like. No, those two creeps were different – more frightening by a mile. I didn't doubt that they were there for a purpose and I had a horrible feeling the purpose was us.

'Who are you and how did you get in?' asked Alex.

The one in the lighter suit took out three business cards and handed one to each of us. On them was printed *Darkstar Programme Security* and a telephone number. There were no names, nothing to identify them individually. I wondered if the backs of their heads would be transparent, like the red-eyed man's.

'We believe,' said the one in the darker suit, 'that you have found Doubleday.'

That name again.

'Who the hell is Doubleday?' said Alex.

The two suited men took no notice of Alex's outburst.

'I believe both of you,' said the lighter suit, looking directly at Becky and me, 'know exactly who I am talking about. Only Alex is unaware of who Doubleday is.'

Alex picked up the phone. 'I am calling the police. You have no right to break in here.'

'Put the phone down, Alex,' said the lighter suit. 'Don't do anything you would come to regret. The police know nothing about Doubleday. But they do know that you three took drugs. Also that you claimed the house was broken into, the bedroom door smashed, that the kitchen was demolished, when obviously it wasn't. As you can see, only two cabinet doors are damaged.'

'The police took pictures, there is evidence,' said Alex.

'You are mistaken,' said the darker suit.

'Drugs can do that,' said the lighter suit.

'We didn't take drugs,' said Alex.

'Whether you did or whether you didn't is entirely up to you three.'

'What do you mean?' said Becky.

'It is simple. Let us know the minute you see Doubleday and I can assure you the whole incident will be struck from police records. All you have to do is call the number on the card.'

They had this strange, antique way of talking, as if by

pronouncing every word properly, no words would be wasted or misunderstood.

'Are you talking about that half-man, half-cyborg thing with red eyes?' I said.

'Precisely.'

'This is a load of rubbish,' said Alex. 'I don't know who you are but I suggest you get out now.'

The dark suit said, 'You wouldn't want another accident to happen to your family, would you, Alex?'

'What do you –' Alex stopped mid-sentence.

'Jake might have drowned. If you don't do as you're asked, your brothers – or even your stepfather – might not be so lucky next time. For instance, Tom could be made to disappear, never to be seen again. You wouldn't want that, would you, Alex?'

Alex dialled 999 on the house phone. The two men didn't move. They stood, waiting. Alex put the phone down. The line was dead.

I followed those two creeps out of the house, watched them climb into their car. It set off fast and noiselessly. As I said, I don't know much about cars, but this one could move.

Alex was in the kitchen, looking pale.

'Are you going to tell me now what the fuck is going on?'

I looked at Becky, hoping that she would tell him. For goodness' sake, Alex of all people deserved the truth, especially after what those two men had said. How could we not tell him about Doubleday? I didn't doubt that he would believe us.

But Becky stalled with a clump of *umm*s and *err*s and so many *aah*s, I felt like throttling her.

'Come on, Becks,' I said. 'Spit it out.'

'All right,' she said at last, and she told Alex how we'd found Doubleday.

She finished, giving me a look as if to say 'that's enough'. She'd left out the portrait. OK, I thought. The portrait could just have been there by coincidence – you know, moons lining up and all that crap. But I didn't believe that for a moment and the more I'd thought about it, the more certain I'd become that the portrait was connected to Doubleday in some way. I mean, I doubt that Doubleday had gone into the pantry for chutney. It was as bare as Old Mother Hubbard's cupboard apart from the painting of Icarus and a pair of shoes. And no, Mr Jones, those shoes didn't belong to Doubleday. I'm no style guru but they didn't go with his outfit.

I was thinking all this when Alex said, 'Anything else I need to know?'

Yes, I thought. Yes.

Becky said, 'No – except this.'

She took the stone from her rucksack and handed it to him. The look of surprise on his face would've been wicked any other time than this. He immediately dropped it, and as he did, it vanished. He was on the verge of saying sorry and stopped. It had reappeared and was lying at his feet. He picked it up, turned it over, studied it.

'Who gave you this?' he asked. Then said, 'No, don't tell me. Let me guess – Icarus.'

The phone rang in the kitchen and we all jumped. Alex picked it up. It was Tom. He listened, was silent for a moment, and then asked how the accident had happened.

Chapter Twenty-Four

I'm not sure I can go on with this.

Mr Jones, I've been trying to imagine that I'm just telling you a story, one that doesn't affect me. But it does. It eats at my soul. I long to find a safe place where I can lock up these memories and throw away the key . . . I'm sorry. It's stupid to cry. It's just that for the last eleven years, I've been walking around with these tin cans rattling behind me. It's a joke, really. Do you know how many job interviews I've been to? Made it to the last two applicants, then, when they realise . . . My past, they tell me, makes me unsuitable. I'm the unreliable witness, my narrative discounted by lawyers, scientists, doctors. In short, they wouldn't trust me with a £10 note. Ten good GCSEs – and I'm grateful to have got a cleaning job at that new tower.

Thanks – that's kind of you. It's a good hanky. I'm afraid I'll make a mess of it.

You do ask the strangest questions, Mr Jones. I don't know if it's good to cry, I only know I don't like crying. I've kept it all in for so long.

Mari has never spoken to me again, not since . . . not since that day. It really hurt, a spoon digging out your insides kind of pain. I tried to explain to her. She said she didn't want to know, she said she wished it was me who had vanished off the face of the earth.

Are you seeing Mari again? I suppose next it'll be the Cleanest Chimney Sweep in Suffolk?

Mark had a rotten time of it, poor bugger. He's quite a recluse these days, lives in a cottage in the middle of nowhere. Who can blame him?

Give me a moment to pull myself together. We're coming to the part that no one believed. My evidence was torn to shreds at the inquest and everyone was convinced I was a fantasist. You'll most probably think the same. Sure you want to hear it?

Chapter Twenty-Five

Those two creeps had been right. Jake was lucky to be alive.

We were all seated around the kitchen table, thinking what to do and failing to come up with a plan, when the phone rang again. This time it was Simon. Alex immediately put him on speaker, so we could all hear Simple Simon's words of wisdom.

'Look, Alex, I overreacted. I thought the kitchen had been totally trashed. Tess and me hadn't had a chance to stop in at the house until we were heading back from Mari's. Two cupboard doors, ridiculous. The police exaggerated the whole incident. I am going to . . . hold on, look, I'll call you back.'

'No, you won't,' said Alex, but Simon was gone.

When I was little, Mr Jones, I was taken on holiday to the seaside. I'd never seen the sea before. I saw these people splashing about in the waves, laughing, and I thought, that's what I want to do. So I just walked into the water – no armbands, no rubber ring, no nothing, sank like a stone. My mum rescued me then, but I think I knew after Simon's call that there was no one to rescue us and the three of us were completely out of our depth.

The logical thing would have been to go back to Mari's, but we couldn't – Alex was too terrified of anything else happening to his family.

Becky said she was going upstairs. When she didn't come down I checked on her. She was fast asleep. I went back to the kitchen, where Alex was busy screwing the cupboard doors back on. I sat at the table and watched him.

He said, 'It's always been like that with Simon. Do you think it's bad that I can't stand my biological father?'

'I don't know,' I said. 'It seems to me you have a great stepdad, that's a plus. And at least you know who your dad is. I've never met mine.'

'Tess shouldn't have tried to blame you.'

'Doesn't matter,' I said. 'My mum blames me for most things – I have tough skin. I come from a dysfunctional one-parent family so I'm used to our lives being laid into by newspapers, politicians and the righteous. That said, I'm glad I have you as a friend.'

Alex looked at me and in that quiet way he had, said, 'I want to be more than that.'

My heart flipped. 'You mean it?'

'Course I do. You're special – come here,' he said.

'What are we going to do?' I said, and he kissed me.

It was only as it was beginning to get dark that the house once more felt uncomfortable, as if every bit of furniture and every curtain was holding its breath, waiting.

'We can't stay here,' said Alex.

'We can't leave,' said Becky coming sleepily down the stairs.

'Why not?'

I spun round. It was Icarus, standing in the hallway.

He took one look at Becky and said: 'Why in the name of Ishmael did you let Doubleday out?'

Icarus listened to our story, then asked to see the cards the two creeps had left.

'Do we call them,' I asked, 'if we see this Doubleday again?'

'No,' said Icarus. 'You mustn't do that.'

'Why not?' I said. 'Who are they?'

'They work for an organisation that monitors all UFO activity. Their job is to make sure that the public never hears about alien contact. Doubleday was a part of Darkstar's flawed experiment with artificial intelligence.'

'How do we know,' I said, 'that you're telling the truth? Who do we trust, in other words? You, who's been convicted of murder? Or a crazy cyborg? Or two sinister guys in dark suits and mirrored glasses?'

I was really getting into my stride when lights came on in the garden. They only do that when there's someone out there.

He was watching us, the barefooted, red-eyed man. Mr Doubleday himself.

Icarus saw him and said, 'All of you, get out now!'

Becky was glued to his side, not moving, watching as Doubleday pushed his face against the glass as if it was water, and walked through it.

Alex and I grabbed Becky. She picked up her rucksack as we pulled her out of the house and we began to run towards

The Jolly Sailor. I was thinking, what if Doubleday should kill Icarus and burn the house down?

'Perhaps,' I said, stopping, gasping for breath, 'it would be best to call those two creeps, get them to sort out this mess.'

I could see Alex was thinking the same thing.

'No, don't,' said Becky. 'If they come they might take Icarus too.'

Alex said, 'You're right – we need to think before we act.'

It felt good when we arrived at the pub – just hearing people talk, doing everyday, normal things.

The barman said, 'Heard the police were called to your house the other night.'

'Yes,' said Becky. 'We thought we saw someone in the garden.'

'How do you know about it?' Alex asked.

'Old John used to work up the local police station when it was in Sudbury. He told us he had heard that it was a lot of fuss about nothing, most probably badgers.'

'Excuse me?' said Becky.

'They can make a hell of a lot of noise. Mrs Fawkes, you know, who works up at the post office, once had a badger come into her cottage through the cat flap. Thought it was a burglar.'

If only, I thought.

We sat in the pub garden. After a while Alex said he'd go back to the house to see if Icarus was all right. That seemed like the stupidest idea I'd heard in a long time.

'You aren't serious?'

'No,' he said. 'I'm not. But we can't stay here.'

'This is a nightmare,' I said.

'You can say that again,' said Alex.

I did.

Alex suggested that he call for a minicab to take us to his boat. Much to my relief, Becky agreed.

We waited outside the pub for about half an hour. When the minicab turned up, it was Mr Seen-It-All Art Lover – just who we didn't need.

'Hope you've got the right money on you this time,' he said.

If I'd been in London I would have told the git to get lost. At least he didn't start on again about Rex Muller.

The road out of Orford wiggles and twists, and then you turn left and head for Woodbridge, past the thatched cottage that I always thought of as the witch's house. After miles, or so it seems, of winding roads, you come to a straight bit and this is Rendlesham Forest. It's really spooky, one of those places you think you wouldn't want to break down in on a dark night. I was always reading in the local paper about a car being written off due to a collision with a deer. They'd never say the deer was a write-off, just the car.

I was thinking this when a man appeared up ahead, our headlights beaming straight onto him. He was in the middle of the road, bent double, no shoes on his feet. He was covered in blood. We all saw him and we all knew who he was. There could be no mistaking Doubleday.

'Don't stop,' Becky screamed. 'Drive on!'

But Mr Know-It-All took no notice and slowed down.

'I'm not going to leave someone in distress. You young

people today, you're all the same – all you ever think about is yourselves. You disgust me.'

'Please – don't stop,' shouted Alex.

Too late. Mr Pomp-and-Pride pulled up and climbed out of his car. To make his point, he slammed the door. Mr Jones, what happened next wasn't from the magic box of cinematic tricks. And I couldn't not look.

The minicab driver walked up to Doubleday. The driver must've known he'd made a terrible mistake. He stopped in his tracks and took off his glasses. Perhaps he thought he was seeing things. We'll never know, because Doubleday lifted him off the ground and threw him across the road. He lay sprawled there. We watched as he crawled to his feet and started to run down the road towards us. Doubleday appeared behind him, put his fist right through him as if he was made of butter. I will never forget the way that minicab driver looked at us, eyes bulging with disbelief.

We scrambled out of the car and ran as fast as we could into the forest, terrified Doubleday would come after us too. He looked in our direction, then climbed into the minicab and drove off. We tried to phone for help, and, yes, Mr Jones, you're right. No signal. There was no point going back to see if the minicab driver was OK, because we knew he was dead. Doubleday had driven over him.

Becky insisted there was nothing to stop us going back to Orford – and Icarus. It took us the rest of the night to get there. I tell you, if nothing else had happened, I would have said that walk was dead creepy. We fell over, scraped and scratched ourselves and it took far longer than we thought it would due to the dark, the trees making shapes of men and beasts, and deers' eyes glinting. By the time we got to the village, the cockerel was awake to welcome us and never had that old bird sounded so sweet.

Afterwards I thought it was for the best that we hadn't been able to call anyone. The house hadn't burned down but Icarus was in the kitchen in a pool of blood, messy as any human's. Becky flipped out and screamed and thought he was dead. She knelt beside him, he took her hand.

'Becky,' he said.

She held his hand to her face and started sobbing. Alex picked up the landline.

'We'll have to call an ambulance.'

Icarus said, 'No, don't. Call Mark. He'll know what to do.'

Alex looked at me.

I said, 'You mean the chimney sweep?'

Chapter Twenty-Six

I found the card Mark had left. As his phone rang, I was trying to think how to explain the reason for calling him so early.

He sounded fully awake and as soon as I said, 'Icarus is here and he's wounded,' he hung up.

Half an hour later, maybe less, he arrived, very calm. He had his toolkit with him, which seemed strange, and once inside the cottage, he put it down, knelt beside Icarus and examined him.

He looked at Becky.

'Where's the stone, Becky? I need the stone.'

'In my rucksack,' she said. 'I'll get it.'

Mark asked Alex to help him take Icarus upstairs. Becky followed them. I was left to clean up the mess – it took ages – but while I was doing it, I thought again about what Mrs Berry had said.

I'd just finished when Becky came down the stairs with Alex and said, 'I don't know what I'll do if he dies.'

'Let's look at that painting again,' I said.

'Why?' she said.

'Because I've had a thought.'

It was in a simple frame, the backing held in place with brown parcel tape. I found a knife and cut carefully along the tape.

'What are you doing?' It was Alex. 'Where did you find that painting?'

'In Mrs Berry's cottage.'

Alex looked at me. 'Is there anything else, Jaz? Anything else I should know?'

'No . . . yes. I'd forgotten about the painting.'

I told Alex everything – where we'd found the painting, the odd stuff Mrs Berry had said, and how it was now beginning to make sense.

It was such a relief. I felt twenty kilograms lighter.

'I fucking wish you'd said all this earlier.'

'So do I,' I said.

Becky said, 'What's happening upstairs? Is he going to live?'

'Yes, it appears so. I don't know what that stone does, do you? No, of course you don't. How did you get us into all this shit, Becky?' Alex got a bottle of lager out of the fridge and took a long swig then said, 'Listen, I overheard Mark talking to Icarus. He said he couldn't protect him much longer.'

'Is that all you heard?' I asked.

'Yes. That's strange enough, isn't it? What are you doing?'

I knew there was something else Alex wasn't telling us. It was written all over his face.

'I want to see if there's anything written on the back of the canvas,' I said as I eased the backing out of the frame. 'Mrs Berry said the painting would be Phoebe's witness, would explain everything.'

On the reverse of the canvas was a label with the artist's name, Phoebe Berry, and the date – nothing else.

'Have you spoken to your mum?' said Becky to Alex.

'I emailed her to say we're OK. What would you suggest I do?'

I started to peel away the label. I don't think I was breathing as I took out a small envelope and unfolded the note inside.

I have it here, Mr Jones. Take it, read it.

If you have found this then you have let him out and heaven help you.

His name is Doubleday. He is a cyborg created by British and American intelligence agencies under the Darkstar Programme to detect the presence of aliens on our planet. Doubleday has evaded his handlers. They had classified him as non-aggressive.

The fools. The utter fools.

Phoebe Berry

Alex was ashen.

'There's something else,' he said.

'What?' I said.

'I heard Mark tell Icarus that we are all in danger, because we know too much and the Darkstar Programme wouldn't hesitate to have us terminated, as they had his brother and his wife.'

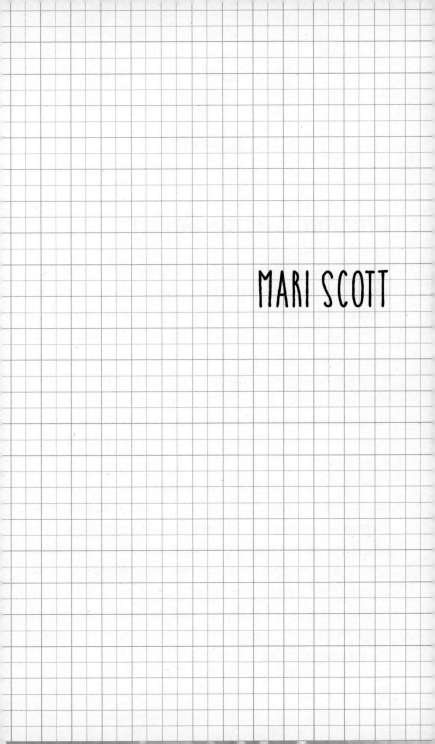

MARI SCOTT

Chapter Twenty-Seven

I spoke to Rex again last night. He told me that after talking to you he had at last been able to untangle the past. He thought it would help me if I talked to you again, Mr Jones, but I doubt it. They say time heals. It hasn't. After all these years the pain is just as bad. His body was never found, you know. I still hope every day for a miracle, that he will turn up alive and well. I can't even bring myself to speak his name. He's everywhere and nowhere, a weight in my heart that won't stop hurting.

So, you said you'd spoken to Jazmin Little. What about Ruth? Simon?

No, I thought not. Simon had two girls with Tess. Yes, he's still married to her. They moved to California, reinvented themselves, wiped out the past. He called me about a year ago to say he had 'found closure'. I bet he has. He's a man with a different hat for every role he's played in his life. First, as my husband and father of Alex; second, as Ruth's husband and father of Becky; third, as Tess's husband and father of the girls. Between roles he has managed to erase all the inconvenient bits.

As for Ruth, hell's bells – where do you start with that narcissistic bitch? After a while, I forgave her – just – for taking Simon from under my nose. By then I'd met Tom and we'd had the twins. But how dare both she and Simon walk out on Becky like that? Abandoning her. I don't give a toss if Ruth was devastated by Simon leaving her. What goes around comes around. She came back for the inquest, loving all the attention, telling the tragic story of her brilliant daughter. Then she got straight back on a plane to India to see her guru.

At the very beginning, I blamed Jazmin Little for everything. I really went for her. We've never spoken since. One day, I would like to. Not yet. Maybe that's progress, I don't know. What I do know is Simon should never have left Jazmin in charge of Becky in the first place.

Well, Jazmin's mother couldn't care less about her. She'd left London and gone to live near her sister in Margate. Mrs Little embellished the truth until the truth was lost. She too relished the publicity, and took the money she'd made selling her story.

I met Icarus, the man in the painting, at a party a couple of months after Phoebe and Frank were killed. He had been living with some travellers in Rendlesham Forest. I recognised him immediately and told him I'd seen Phoebe's portrait of him. He said he'd sat for her about a year earlier, after he'd met her and Skye on the beach at Shingle Street.

Maybe it was because he'd known Phoebe, but I was instantly attracted to him. We drank a lot, smoked a lot, and when Icarus told me he was from another planet on the edge of our solar system and that he had been sent to earth by his president in order to understand love, I half believed him. He made anything sound possible. He showed me his notebooks full of crazy writing and asked if I understood it.

I told him they were gobbledygook as far as I was concerned.

He said there was a formula for the survival of all species and if it wasn't followed, everything would eventually die. His own race was in danger of becoming extinct, like the dinosaurs. When I said the dinosaurs became extinct because an asteroid hit the earth, Icarus said if I truly believed that then I didn't understand the power of love. He said that he was only beginning to, and that love was the most extraordinary force the human race possessed. It marked us out from all other alien species and was the reason for our survival. Without it, he said, we'd be nothing more than dinosaurs.

He'd come up with a formula – it went like this:

Love plus passion equals imagination.
Love plus imagination equals creation.
Love plus creation equals life.
Love plus life equals time.
Love plus time equals death.

But, he said, nothing exists without love. And that's what his race didn't have: the ability to feel the most vital of emotions.

That summer I saw a lot of him. It was as if he'd hypnotised me. I'd fallen in love with him and told him so.

He said he felt something for me but didn't know what it was, and then, in September, he left to go travelling. I went to the Slade School of Art to study painting and sculpture and that's where I met Ruth.

Yes, I did. I saw him once again. This is difficult to say . . . I haven't told anybody this before.

Mr Jones, I lied when I told the court the last time I saw Icarus was that September.

Perhaps because I felt guilty. Because if I'd reported what had happened to me to the police, then Lazarus and Skye might still have been alive.

Icarus turned up at the Slade on a warm June day the following year. He said he would like to take me home. I thought he was joking when he took me to St Paul's Cathedral. I asked if he was going to tell me he was an angel. He said something about transport being unable to pick me up from the ground. I thought, oh, here we go again. Since I'd last seen him I'd grown up and I'd begun to think of him as a bit of a nutcase.

We climbed the 376 steps to the Stone Gallery – it goes all the way round the outside of the dome. He wanted to go higher to the Golden Gallery but I got vertigo and couldn't move from the door that led outside – I just wanted to get back down. Icarus leaned over the railing and I told him to be careful, he might fall.

He said, 'I already have.' He turned finally and looked at me for a long time. Then he said, 'Mari, I'm so sorry. I wish it could be you.'

I said, 'You're mad,' and I ran down those 376 steps as if I was being chased by the devil. Icarus didn't come after me. And that, Mr Jones, was the last time I saw him.

He pushed Skye and Lazarus off the Golden Gallery. It was only when I saw his photo on the front page of the newspapers three years later that I remembered that he had asked me to jump with him. I was too ashamed to tell Rex. So I told no one.

Icarus was sent to prison and I thought he would remain behind bars until he died. Too late, I found out that prison bars couldn't hold him, that Alex, Becky and Jazmin had met him. Alex called me and said that he and the girls were going to London. I didn't think anything of it. I was so worried about Jake. He had broken his leg very badly . . . Oh, Mr Jones, I'm wrong to be so angry with Jazmin, I know that. But the person I am most furious with is myself. It was so easy at the time to blame her – after all, everyone else did. The simple, terrible truth is, I didn't speak up when I could have done.

Do you know how often I think about . . . oh, lord, sorry, I don't mean to cry . . . all these years, it's been driving me crazy. I wake up some mornings and think I will go to London and tell Jazmin that I'm sorry, truly sorry that I didn't speak up . . . but I can't.

JAZMIN LITTLE

Chapter Twenty-Eight

I was just about to leave a note to tell you I'm off, and to say I'm sorry but I won't be able to see you again. And here you are. I'm pleased you came, Mr Jones.

No, I am, I'm really pleased. I feel we have unfinished business.

I thought you might not want to hear any more from me after I became a blubbering wreck.

Did you see Mari?

No doubt she told you I was unreliable and totally responsible for what happened.

I wanted to tell you in person my side of the story after Icarus was wounded, after Doubleday had killed the minicab driver. After I discovered the letter. Maybe if I tell it the way I remember it, I'll have some peace at last.

You know, you've never answered a single one of my questions. But I want to ask you this: how does anyone know who is the villain and who is the goodie? Many see me as the villain. But where does that leave Icarus? Maybe we are all responsible for what happened, every one of us.

I was thinking recently about barbed wire. It was invented by an American for cattle, way back in the days of old. Should he be held accountable for its use in concentration camps? What I am trying to ask is this: am I the baddie, or was it Icarus who caused the death of Skye and Lazarus, and . . . oh, sorry, here I go again.

But it's not only Becky's death that's screwed me up. I keep not mentioning it, walking round it – a bloody dinosaur that doesn't even fit in the room, makes elephants look manageable. The bit that tears me up is, I don't know what happened. No one believed that, no one.

That's another hanky I owe you, Mr Jones. You see, the thing is, I loved – I love – will love no one else. I'm like a wood pigeon – paired for life. He loved me, I know he did. I would give *anything* – anything to see him again.

Oh, thank you – tea with a bit of sugar. Sorry, this is all much harder . . . The trouble is, none of these wounds have healed. When I remember it, I'm there, right back there. Ask me what I did yesterday and I haven't a clue.

Give me a moment, then I'll carry on . . .

OK.

After Icarus was wounded, Mark stayed with him until tea-time the next day. Becky was with them most of the time, and Alex and me sat cuddled up in the sitting room, wondering what we were going to do.

'Surely by now,' I said, 'someone must've noticed that Icarus has escaped from the open prison. Electric bells ringing, wardens running, police road blocks, that kind of thing – high drama.'

We looked on the news. There was nothing.

Mark came down the stairs.

'I'm taking Icarus away,' he said.

'Away where?' said Alex and me together.

'Back to prison, I hope,' I added. 'Before he pushes someone else off St Paul's.'

Alex looked worried. 'What about us?' he said. 'What if Doubleday decides that the way to get to Icarus is to use Becky, and turns up here?'

I could tell by Mark's expression that this had become very messy indeed for the Cleanest Chimney Sweep in Suffolk.

Before Mark could answer, I realised Icarus had come quietly into the room, Becky at his side. He looked surprisingly well, drop-dead handsome – and I wouldn't have trusted him with a pet budgerigar.

'I didn't push Skye and Lazarus from the Golden Gallery,' he said to me. 'I helped them.'

'Didn't that amount to the same thing?' I said.

'If they had fallen, yes. But they didn't. Our craft collected them.'

I wasn't quite buying all this. Or rather, I did, but only when Icarus was talking to me, when his dark eyes were on me.

'Why didn't you go with them?'

'Because then our whole mission would have failed.'

I was hoping that Mark would say, 'Come off it Icarus, not that old horse chestnut,' but he didn't.

He said, 'Alex is right. It isn't safe here for any of you.'

'Who are you?' I asked Mark.

'Look . . . it's not important who I am,' said Mark. 'There isn't time to explain. You have to trust me, you'll all have to trust me. I've planned how I'm going to get Icarus out of here.'

This was made to look very different at the inquest. I was accused of being the ringleader but I wasn't. If I am honest, I wanted us to go back to Mari and Tom's. But Icarus said if Doubleday found us there he could cause a lot of harm and his handlers would make sure of one thing – that the incident wasn't reported. Mark told us they had carte blanche from the British and American governments. No questions asked. I could see Alex thinking about his family.

Becky said, 'I'm not leaving Icarus.'

So that put the kibosh to Mark's plan of taking Icarus away from there by himself.

It was dusk. We hadn't yet turned on the lights, and the room lit up neon blue as a police car sped past with its light flashing. It felt like a warning. Time to go.

Mark had parked his van round the back of the house. He said he'd take us to Ipswich station. Becky and me grabbed a few possessions and we all climbed in the van. Mark turned on the radio as we drove off and if we were in any doubt about leaving, what we heard put an end to it. The local news was reporting that a punk with a mohican had stolen a police car. An unidentified, mutilated body had been found in Rendlesham Forest but the two incidents were not thought to be related.

'We should go to London,' said Icarus.

I remembered that I still had the keys to my mum's old flat

in Camden. As long as no one had moved in, we could hang out there for a while.

'Not for long,' I said.

'But long enough,' said Icarus.

It went hard against me in court. I've thought about what other options there were. Oh my word, haven't I thought about it. The big dipper of possibilities has rolled and coasted through my head and still does. That bloodied path not taken.

I didn't wholly trust the Cleanest Chimney Sweep in Suffolk. I had a feeling he was playing both sides. I changed my mind at the inquest, especially after they did what they did to him. If I thought I'd had it bad, it was nothing compared to what they did to his testimony.

We sat in the back of the van and Becky rested her head on Icarus's shoulder. She looked exhausted.

Mark said he wanted to stop in Ipswich and we made a detour to a party shop. He knocked on the side door and came out with these animal onesies, brand new, still in their packets.

'Put them on,' he said.

'Come on, man,' said Alex. 'You are kidding. Everyone will look at us.'

Mark said, 'But they will only remember the animal suits, not who was in them. Believe me. Now, hurry.'

Mine was a zebra suit, Alex's a fox, Icarus's a tiger, and Becky's a black cat.

I thought it was a potty idea but Mark wasn't listening to any of it. He said when we got to London we should throw them away as soon as we were out of Liverpool Street Station. And that we were to ring him once a day on a cheap mobile he gave us. I wondered how it was that Mark was so good at all this spook stuff.

Actually, I quite liked wearing that zebra suit. It was a chilly summer's night when we caught the train to London. We arrived late at Liverpool Street Station where we fitted in perfectly: just some crazy students out on a wild one.

Chapter Twenty-Nine

The Darwin Estate where I grew up couldn't have been better named – only the fittest survived there. It's not in the posh part of Camden, more round the corner near Kentish Town. It was a bit of a gamble but I couldn't see anyone moving into my mum's pokey two-bedroom flat in a hurry, and fortunately I was right. It was empty except for the smell of stale tobacco and a pile of junk mail. It looked dead strange without furniture. There were patches of bright blue carpet where the furniture had been while the rest had faded. The fridge stank like the inside of a dosser's mouth. The only thing that could be said in the flat's favour was that it had running water.

Becky said, 'Hell's bells, Jaz – I didn't realise it was this bad.'

That made me laugh. I mean, we were better off than some but that's not saying much. If the rich can't see it, can't smell it, it can't bother them. They don't know such places exist except in a gritty TV drama.

'Welcome to Planet Grunge,' I said. 'It's not that bad.'

'You're joking,' said Becky.

. . .

Here I need to say something, Mr Jones, because it's important. That first night in the flat there was nothing to sleep on and I said, a bit like a bossy matron, that Becky and me should have one room, and Alex and Icarus could have the other.

It was Becky who said, 'Come on, do you think I'm that stupid? It's obvious you and Alex are an item, and I'm really happy for you. And I want to be with Icarus. I need to be with Icarus.'

Icarus hadn't let go of Becky's hand since we got on the train and I was too bushwhacked to say anything more. But I was glad that Alex and I would sleep together.

At the inquest, Ruth said she should never have let that piece of scum into their lives. That piece of scum, by the way, was me.

The next day we went to an internet cafe. Becky had the log-in for Ruth's account at a department store and she ordered beds, duvets, a table and chairs, TV, everything, and did one of her yah-yah I-want-it-now tantrums and it all arrived the same day.

Our old neighbour from flat fifty didn't miss a thing. Mrs Mankell was the reverse side of the Mrs Sunshine coin.

'You back then?' she said, as if there was dog shit on my shoes. 'Won the bleeding lottery, have you?'

'I'm staying here for a bit,' I said.

Her head bobbed this way and that, trying to see beyond me into the narrow hallway. 'Got people staying with you, then?'

'What are you?' I said. 'The bloody Gestapo? We never stuck our noses into your doings, now leave us alone.'

'Any noise and I'll be calling the police,' she said.

'I doubt that. You wouldn't want those sniffer dogs going through your boy's pyjamas.'

That was enough. She slouched back to her flat and slammed her door.

I said to the others that I didn't know how long it would be until the police or the council or both came knocking.

Icarus said, 'We'll be gone in a week.'

We. I didn't like the sound of that.

'Gone where?' I said.

'Home,' said Icarus.

We were sitting at our new table, eating an Indian takeaway.

I looked at Alex in the hope that he would say something like 'no'. No, you are not taking my sister anywhere. It dawned on me a sentence too late that Icarus had been talking to Alex and Becky while I'd been cleaning up the flat and getting the takeaway.

'Jazmin,' said Icarus, 'I know you are scared and I understand. I promise you, all will be well.'

Perhaps when aliens promise you something, you shouldn't take it too seriously. I don't think they understand the concept of a promise. Still, it didn't stop Icarus from sounding believable – he was very good at that. When I was with him, everything had a logic to it.

But I'm running away with myself. Back to the chicken korma.

I looked out of the window to avoid his eyes and said, 'I've had enough of your airy-fairy alien crap. Tell us what you're doing, and what you want from us.'

173

Icarus put down his fork and told us that he came from a planet that wasn't affected by Earth time.

'We look the same as you but we don't age and we don't suffer death – eventually we fade away. We tolerate each other but on the whole we prefer our own company. We teach our children to be considerate, but we have no feeling for them and they have none for us. Slowly my race is fading away. Technically, we are more advanced than you but the one thing that we have been unable to artificially create is love. Without love there is no desire to keep reproducing. There is no music, no art, no literature.

'Three of us were chosen for the mission to bring this emotion back to our planet: Troyon, Ishmael and myself. I see now that we were naive in the extreme. The impact of our crash landing in Rendlesham Forest killed Troyon. Our craft's mortuary had been damaged and Ishmael and I agreed we should leave Troyon's body in the forest rather than take it home as is our way. We buried him there. When we returned to the craft, men in uniform were coming towards us. Ishmael went to greet them; I stayed back and watched as he was taken away. Our crew did enough repairs to take the craft out of there and we returned the next night. I dropped our stones for Ishmael in case he was unable to find us.'

'Like the stone you gave me,' said Becky.

'Yes,' said Icarus and took it out of his pocket. It pulsated with light. 'The stone can heal, regenerate, and its magnetic power draws our people to it.'

'It healed Becky?' asked Alex.

'Yes.'

'Wait,' I said. 'This Troyon – surely you could have used one of your stones on him?'

'No. He was dead. It is forbidden by our laws to do such a thing.'

'Like "Do Not Resuscitate",' I said. 'But what I don't understand is, why has it taken you this long to decide to go home?'

'Because I had to learn how to love. I had to understand what it feels like – the amazement of knowing that you are not alone, that there is someone you would give your life for. Becky has taught me how to love.'

'Perhaps you're better off without love,' said Alex. 'Look what us humans have done in the name of love – love of religion, of country, of money. Most of the time it's just an excuse to be greedy or cruel. We say we do it in the name of love.'

'Tell me, Alex,' said Icarus, 'would you rather be free of emotion and feel nothing for Jazmin?'

Alex looked at me and my cheeks burned. 'No,' he said. 'I wouldn't give up this feeling for all the world.'

And I knew he meant it.

Chapter Thirty

The next day Becky wanted to go for a walk with me. Icarus looked out of the window.

I could see he wasn't sure it was a good idea.

Neither was Alex.

'We need food,' I said. 'We'll be gone for two hours, max.'

I couldn't wait to get out of that flat.

Icarus insisted that we took the stone so he would be able to find us if necessary.

'What are we going to do for money, Jaz?' said Becky as we neared Camden Lock.

That two thousand pounds hung heavy with me and made my relationship with Becky not altogether honest, unbalanced the seesaw.

I took a deep breath and, expecting the worst, told her what Simon had done.

'Good,' she said. 'You must keep it.'

'You're not cross?'

'Why should I be? It's what Simple Simon always does. He

throws money at what he doesn't understand and after that everyone understands for him.'

I took some cash from the machine, though later I wondered if that had been a foolish thing to do. I'd just given away our whereabouts.

It was a bright, sunny day and seeing so many people milling around, all relatively normal, doing normal things, made me think – how did it come to this, being stuck in my mum's flat with an alien?

After we'd done the food shopping we went to a cafe by the canal and ordered two slices of red velvet cake and a pot of tea. We sat in the sunlight and watched two ducks argue over a crust of bread.

'Are you going to go through with this?' I asked.

'What do you mean by "this"?' said Becky.

'I mean, are you going to go with Icarus?'

'Yes, absolutely yes.'

Suddenly the cake wasn't so delicious, the sun was too hot, the ducks too noisy.

'You're going to give all this up to go goodness knows where? You have a life, a career. Look how well your book is selling. *The Martian Winter* is still in all the bookshops.'

'Jaz, I never wanted any of that to happen. No – wait, let me finish. Ruth wanted me to be a writer, she wanted to show off her clever daughter. My father enjoyed saying his princess was an author – and look where that led him: to the Queen of Bitches. They never once asked me what *I* wanted, never. You have been my one and only friend, the best friend I've ever had.'

I did interrupt then. I said, 'You accused me of not understanding you.'

'Sorry, Jaz – I was angry, that was all. I didn't mean it. But I do mean it when I say that if I lost Icarus, I would lose myself.'

'No, you wouldn't – that's pathetic.'

'What is there to anchor me here?' said Becky. 'Apart from you and Alex, nothing. I think the question should be, why do you want to stay? Jump with us, Jaz.'

That shocked me. 'You mean, trust everything Icarus says and jump into oblivion like Skye and Lazarus?'

'Why not? Nothing is certain, nothing is set in concrete. Anyway, what do you have going for you here?'

'I've got Alex,' I said, but Becky didn't seem to hear.

'Look at all these people,' said Becky. 'Look at all the shopping. What are they buying? Nothing but a hope that tomorrow will be better than today because they have a new dress. That's what I call pathetic. Leaving with Icarus is brave.'

I sat looking at the sun ripple on the water and I realised that for the first time I felt jealous of her. Up to that point, I never had. She was right, she had far more courage than me. Without knowing it, we had reached a crossroads. Already I felt left behind.

'Why aren't I like you?' I said.

'If you were, we would never have been friends.'

'You always tell me that Icarus is like you.'

'He is and he isn't. We are learning together and I don't care where the journey takes us. Come on, Jaz, don't look so sad.'

Perhaps it was then that it dawned on me that without Becky, my life would have been black and white and grey all over.

'You are richer in your soul,' she said.

'That sounds like Icarus babble,' I said.

Becky stared down at her cup.

Jealousy isn't a pretty emotion. 'I'm sorry,' I said. 'That was mean.'

Becky leaned over and took my hand. 'Love you, Jaz.'

We were about to leave when Becky said, 'There's one thing I'd like to do.'

She dragged me into the covered market to Mary May, Fortune Teller to the Stars.

'Becky, don't be crazy. It's a waste of dosh.'

She took no notice. 'Come on, Jaz, let's give it a go.'

We had to wait, sitting on creaky plastic chairs. It was a grungy-looking place. I suppose it made all the drivel that Mary May had to say feel more real.

I whispered to Becky, 'Nobody believes the future is hidden in here.'

That's what I thought then. Now I'm not so sure.

Becky went first and insisted I was there for her reading. The room was so dingy, hung with saris, and smelling of joss sticks. It was hard to make out Mary May in the gloom. I reckon she must have been about ninety. She looked more alien than an alien. I sat in another plastic chair against the wall while Mary May spent ages studying Becky's hand. Then she sprang back, looking really shocked.

'What is it?' said Becky.

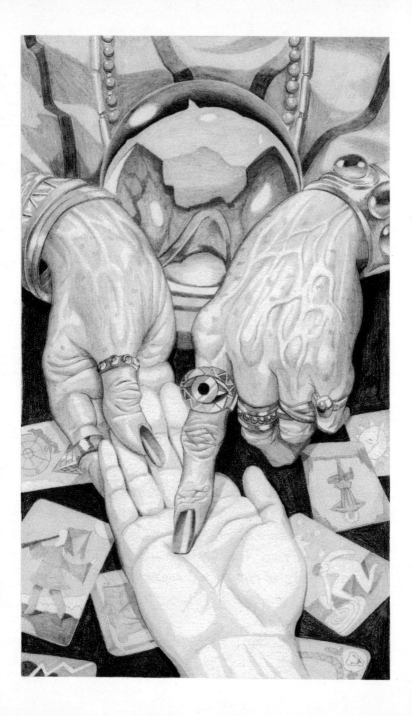

I was certain Mary May had seen that Icarus was up to no good. I bit the inside of my mouth, crossed my fingers and hoped this might be a turning point. At last Becky would see she was being conned.

'You and the man you love are going on a journey,' said Mary May. 'A journey that no one – no one of this world – has taken before. I see you have made your decision – you will jump.'

That gave me the shivers.

The old lady patted Becky's hand. 'You're a lucky girl,' she said. 'Very lucky.' Then she looked at me. 'Come here, dear. Let's see what your future holds.'

'No, thanks,' I said, standing up. 'I don't want to.'

Becky said, 'You can't get out of it now, Jaz. I'll wait outside.'

I sat down and reluctantly gave over my hand. Mary May said a lot of hocus-pocus; perhaps it was to sweeten the pill, I don't know.

Then she looked at me sadly and said, 'You're going to lose the boy you love and you will . . .'

I snatched my hand away and didn't wait to hear what else she had to say.

'That was quick,' said Becky.

'It's all a load of rubbish,' I said.

We walked back along the canal, me trying not to think about the fortune teller, Becky enjoying what she'd been told.

'Becks,' I said.

She turned to look at me and the sun caught her hair, which was pushed back from her face. I thought she looked beautiful. I saw her as an astronaut, about to go on a voyage from which there was no return.

'Nothing,' I said.

She carried on walking in front of me and I was glad she didn't see me well up.

When I'm very down these days, I think of those few hours. She was my best friend. Irreplaceable. Gone.

Chapter Thirty-One

The flat was small, I grant you that, and the mini heat-wave didn't help – even with the windows open the rooms were baking. But it wasn't either of those factors that made it claustrophobic, as if we were cooped-up battery hens waiting for slaughter. It was the arrival of the two suited men two days later.

It was too hot to sleep. I remember the clock said five in the morning as I wandered into the kitchen to get a glass of water. I was standing by the sink, letting the tap run while staring out onto the graffitied dustbin sheds, when I saw them. They were standing in exactly the same pose, wearing mirrored sunglasses, one otherwise identical suit slightly darker than the other. They were looking up at me. I fetched Alex, who was not best pleased to be woken so early. He looked sleepily out of the lounge window and then stepped back quickly.

'Shit,' he said. 'What are they doing here?'

'I don't think they've come to tell us we've won the lottery, that's for shizzle.'

I jumped. Icarus had quietly materialised behind us.

'I thought we'd have longer,' he said.

He sounded despondent.

'Those are the two characters from central casting who came to the house in Orford,' I said.

'They are Doubleday's handlers,' said Icarus.

Becky was up now too. She wrapped her arms around Icarus. 'Handlers? Where?' she said. 'How did they find us?'

The cashpoint in Camden Town, I thought.

'How did they lose Doubleday in the first place?' said Alex.

'Doubleday is a hybrid,' said Icarus. He paused. 'He was constructed using Troyon's body.'

Icarus dropped his head. I had seen him look worried but never before had I seen him look sad.

'Troyon was rare in our race. He possessed more empathy than Ishmael or me. He had been chosen to find and understand this emotion, love. His death put the operation in jeopardy. I was instructed to take his place.'

'It sounds to me as if you cared for him,' I said, 'and your people are supposed to feel no love for anything or anybody.'

'We are kind to each other. We are not a cruel race, not like humans. Ishmael is one of our wise men. I helped him but I failed Troyon. I led Ishmael out of the citadel back to our craft in the forest and there, to my surprise, he ordered me to stay on Earth and learn about love. Ishmael was second in command and I had to obey. It's only now that I love that I know how much I miss Ishmael and mourn Troyon. Lazarus's brother Rex reminded me of Troyon – a kind, gentle man. That was why I let him paint my portrait.'

'Do you know how Doubleday got away?'

Icarus shook his head.

'All I know is that he fooled his handlers and escaped their control.' He paused. 'Then he came for me.'

'So why was this cyborg locked in Mrs Berry's pantry?' I asked.

'It was only after the accident that killed Phoebe and Frank that I learned what Doubleday was. What was left of Troyon's mind had been corrupted and, as Doubleday, he blamed me for all that had happened to him, for not taking his body home. His mind was focused, set on a single thought: he needed a stone to make him whole again. But it would never have worked.'

'Why not?' I asked.

'Our stones made clay flesh, a dead boy come alive, but they couldn't give either Skye or Lazarus the essence of humanity. They lacked all sense of love. A stone wouldn't work on something that was part electrical circuits. Doubleday was out of control, he was a danger, he had to be stopped. The portrait and the shoes fooled him into thinking I was in the pantry, and lured him in. Darkness was the only way to immobilise him.'

What hadn't been said still hung there. If those two creeps from central casting were Doubleday's handlers, where the hell was Doubleday?

Now call me old-fashioned, Mr Jones, but I like to know who we should be rooting for, so I asked Icarus, 'The two men out there – good or bad?'

'They are bad.'

'And while we're on it . . . when did you meet Mark? And what is he to you?'

Becky interrupted me. 'Jaz, leave it. Come on, why are you asking all these questions? It's not helping.'

But Icarus seemed unfazed. 'The day I was sent for trial Mark was assigned to me.'

'So they knew by then that you were an alien?'

'Yes. But no one else was ever to find out. The Darkstar Programme's business is to make sure you, the people of this planet, are kept ignorant of what is out there.'

'Doubleday – is he a part of the Darkstar Programme?' I said.

'Yes, Jaz, don't be thick, you know he is,' said Becky. 'You heard those guys.'

Icarus said, 'Doubleday was the first cyborg, the most advanced piece of engineering on Earth.'

'Not the universe?' I said.

Icarus smiled. 'You don't believe this is the only inhabited planet?'

'Not many aliens have called in to say hello,' I said.

'The Darkstar Programme has been making contact with other alien life-forms for over forty-five years. Doubleday was created to be used in war and terrorist situations.'

Then, just when I thought that maybe I would be able to pass stage one in alien-cyborg physics, everything went creepy again.

Becky started to talk to Icarus quietly in a language I'd never heard before.

'Hold on,' I said. 'What are you saying?'

Becky seemed almost surprised I hadn't understood.

'Just that I'll be glad when we're out of here.'

I think, Mr Jones, that was the first time I realised how deep the love between them was and began to understand something of what Becky had said about not needing a code.

I said to Alex, when we were alone, 'Who do we trust? Who?'

'You,' he said. 'I trust you. After all this is over – whatever the over is – would you consider, Ms Little, living with me on my humble houseboat?'

'Yes,' I said and I kissed him. 'And yes and yes again.' And I kissed him again.

Later, we called Mark, told him that Doubleday's handlers had turned up. He said he needed to speak to Icarus.

I'd a vague hope that the gang that roamed the Darwin Estate might deal with the creeps. They would be fresh pickings for the bullyboys. I watched them circle the two men, then the gang leader went up to them. He was a prize bruiser, all cocky walk and cocky talk. He got within feet of them when, to my surprise and his, he fell backwards. He stood up, looking stunned and didn't return for a second bout. I wondered then if Doubleday's handlers were cyborgs too.

'Don't they ever need a loo break?' said Becky.

'Apparently not,' I said.

'They must do. They must eat and drink.'

'Are they even human?'

The two men made Icarus even more watchful. No more shopping trips for us. Icarus stayed awake, and when he wasn't with us he was with Becky in their room.

•••

Lying in the dark that night, I said to Alex, 'It's not too late for us to leave. We could phone your mum and Tom, tell them what's going on. They'd come and get us.'

'I've been thinking about that but we can't. What if anything happened to them? And Becky wouldn't come. She has her heart set on going with Icarus.'

'Do you believe him when he talks about his planet?' I said. 'Because I don't know.'

Alex took my hand. 'Hey, Jaz, think about it. If you had a chance to start again in the Garden of Eden, wouldn't you take it and make a better world? Not make the same idiotic mistakes we've made here? Look at the mess we're in.'

'But we only have Icarus's word about the place he comes from. He could just be feeding us a baloney sandwich. And he's going to take Becky back to his den and eat her up. It's not like we can call and ask, "How are you liking it there? Email some photos."'

I nestled my head in the crook of Alex's neck.

'Do you really believe that?' he said.

'No. Maybe. Yes.'

'If I phoned Mum,' said Alex, 'it would end with Icarus being rearrested.'

I know it sounds disloyal, but I said, 'Would that really be so bad?'

We'd been there for four days and four nights. That was all the time I'd had to relish that lovely, expensive furniture. Four days and four nights to try to talk some sense into Becky's unworldly head. I really tried.

'It's not like going to Paris or New York where you can jump on a plane home if you don't like it. BA doesn't offer an intergalactic service yet.'

'I know that, I know,' she said.

There was no reasoning with her. But I'd known that all along.

I turned on the TV. It was showing an ancient video of The Monkees. The trouble was, I wasn't a believer.

Becky came into our room on the fifth night, weeping. Icarus had gone. Alex went to look. He wasn't in the flat and fortunately neither was anybody else. We checked outside and the two suited men weren't there either. I thought, what if they've taken him? And immediately I felt as if a great weight had been lifted from us. Perhaps I'd been wrong. Perhaps Icarus was a gent and had decided to go it alone. Becky was inconsolable. I thought I could cope with that. But after a night of her weeping and wailing, telling us she'd rather die than live without him, I wasn't so sure anyone could handle, let alone live with, her heartbreak.

When we heard footsteps in the hall the next morning we all froze.

I was certain that Doubleday's handlers were back and had broken in. Alex stood ready to defend us, then Icarus walked into the room. We must have looked like a bunch of startled deer.

He said, 'I have to leave tonight.'

'What shall we do?' I said.

'You must stay here. You have all done more than enough

for me. I've called Mark – he'll pick you up tonight after I've left.'

Becky went to him.

'I'm staying with you, you know that.'

'It's too dangerous, Becky,' he said. 'I can't risk it.'

'I love you,' she said.

You know those sugary, sticky moments in films, when the music plays and the couple embrace. Well, no music played, just the couple embraced. It was then that I saw Icarus was crying.

He said, 'I've waited so long to know what love is. The idea of being parted from you, Becky, is unbearable. It physically hurts me. But no, my love, it isn't safe.'

'Nothing is,' said Becky. 'And I'm not letting you go without me.'

What the hell can anyone say to such marshmallow sentiments?

On the news that morning there was a picture of Icarus. They had aged him up but not so much that he wasn't recognisable. The news presenter said that Icarus was a youthful-looking man in his early forties.

'You don't look more than twenty-three,' said Alex.

'It doesn't matter, it's still me.'

The presenter went on to say that Icarus was extremely volatile, that he was a suspected murderer with links to a terrorist organisation and was on the run. On no account should the general public approach him.

What do the French say? *Fait accompli*? It was fate, all right, and it was complicated.

Becky wrote a letter to Ruth and Simon explaining her decision. She took great care to make her points. She stressed that me and Alex could have done nothing to prevent what was about to happen and that we were in no way to blame. She also said that there was no way back once she had gone. She read it aloud. It sounded so final, I felt a lump in my throat.

Icarus even wrote a bit at the bottom. I folded it up and put it somewhere safe. When it was dark, they left, taking nothing with them.

I had never seen Becky look as happy as she did when she said goodbye. She was positively alight with love.

She kissed me and told me not to be sad. 'I'm going on the greatest adventure.'

Those were her last words to me. After what happened, I gave the letter to the police. They lost it. Then they said they'd never had it in the first place. Alex wasn't there, I was the only one left – my narrative dismissed.

I'm sorry, Mr Jones, I don't want to talk any more today.

MATRON OF ST MARY'S HOSPICE, CUMBRIA

Chapter Thirty-Two

Are you a relation, Mr Jones? A friend?

No, Mark has had no visitors – you're the first. And I'm afraid you'll be the last. The doctors don't think he will make it through the night. He was brought in a week ago. He'd been managing by himself and had refused all treatment up to then. Would you like to see him?

We are a small hospice and do our best to keep a family feel to the place. Unfortunately tonight we are very short staffed. When did you last see him? That was some time ago. He will have changed considerably. This is his room, he's asleep. Do you want to stay here until he wakes? Good, that will be most helpful. Often the dying just need company. I always say that death is like birth, only in reverse. If you need anything, don't hesitate to ring the bell.

I think I should warn you, Mr Jones, that the patient has been saying some very peculiar things. The dying often do. I wouldn't take any notice. Jumbled-up memories, you know, not in any order. Would you like the door left open or shall I close it?

Well, then. I'll check with you in about half an hour.

MARK KEELE

Chapter Thirty-Three

I know you. I've met you before – just can't place you. Jones, you say? No, that's not right – that's not your name.

Where was it . . . ? It was a long time ago, a different life. It's the drugs, I didn't want the drugs.

Icarus fell out of the sky. You're not Icarus, I knew him. I've been thinking a lot about him. Are you an alien too? Take off your sunglasses – let me see your eyes.

Don't leave – please don't leave. I need to talk. Everyone here thinks I'm away with the fairies. You see, my blood is poisoning me, killing me.

Bentwaters airbase . . . I thought that was why you'd come . . . maybe you are an angel.

Yes . . . strange what you never forget. Never. Even drugged up to the hilt of non-existence I can remember that time well. I was a technician in the labs, down, down, down, three floors down, under the base. Smelled of stale air.

Christmas Day . . . that day he came down. Icarus, a gift from outer space. Didn't know it then. I was with my brother Frank and his girlfriend Phoebe at her mother's house in Orford. I'd been living with them. Good times. Hot summer, friends, artist's life, still full of possibilities. That evening, driving back to Shingle Street, we saw the lights . . . Frank joked . . . my boyhood wish had come true . . . the aliens had landed. Phoebe said it was just the lighthouse – it was a misty night. I had a phone call from a friend . . . said something was happening in Rendlesham Forest.

Frank and Phoebe had had a difficult year. Wanted children.

Do you have them, Mr Jones – children?

I can't hear you. Did you speak? Thought not. Noisy. It's noisy in my head. I can see all this as if it was a film. Perhaps that's all we are when we die, just a film going frame by frame until we run out of images.

Phoebe had suffered a miscarriage in . . . in the month of leaves. October, Nov . . . November. It was November. The sculpture of the little girl was a way for her to deal with her grief. Their grief.

Boxing Day, called back to the airbase. God, I hated that place. Hated it more when the Chief of Security asked me to sign another Official Secrets Act. Already signed about half a dozen before they'd given me the job. This was different though . . . If I ever spoke of what I had seen I would be terminated. Meaning, I'd be discreetly executed. At the very bottom, in small print, were the words 'Darkstar Programme'.

Military work was well paid. Saw the job as a step up the ladder. There were one – two – three – four – six of us on my usual team. That day there were twenty-five and I knew none of them. I asked what was going on and was told it was an inappropriate question.

I don't think I can say more. Mouth too dry. Pour me a pint, Mr Jones . . .

You still here? Good. Must've fallen asleep. Yes, of course – my mind hasn't gone yet. Where . . . that's right, Boxing Day. They'd caught an alien who'd landed in a craft in Rendlesham Forest . . . he was being held in the observation room. I was called in to have a look at him. Don't know what I had been expecting . . . pointy head, triangular eyes; whatever it was, this wasn't it. Before me was a man dressed in a fancy costume, more eighteenth century than of our time. Incredibly elegant. I thought it was a joke . . . except no one was laughing. He was classified as having 'Abilities Unknown'.

What was that, Mr Jones?

Yes, yes, you're right, I monitored him and noted my observations. The alien had said he was known as Ishmael. He sat in a chair, eyes closed, never moving.

It was about midnight on 28th December when I realised Ishmael had vanished from the holding cell. He must have walked through the walls because he was standing right behind me.

He said, 'Don't speak, Mark.'

Yes . . . knew my name. The dials on the desk in front of me had stopped moving. The main lights flickered. That's when I saw him – another alien; he came through a steel door as if it didn't exist. I saw his eyes, the way he looked at me, the way he knew me. Knew all about me.

He said, 'I am Icarus.'

Unable to move, I watched as the aliens walked together through the closed steel door.

I was found unconscious on the floor. I asked about Ishmael and was told that everything was under control. I was to go home and wait until I was called. I wanted to know more but those officers don't get medals answering questions. They get medals muddling up answers. For some reason I never understood, I didn't tell them about Icarus and they never asked.

It was only when I arrived back at Phoebe and Frank's that I realised I'd been away for three days. A cold, misty morning. That's right. The sky was magnificent . . . ice blues thrown across a grey sea . . . I remember I went into the studio to see if the sculpture was finished. The plinth was empty, Phoebe's tools scattered on the floor. It felt strange. I went to make a cup of tea and in the hall I saw clay footprints. I told myself it was impossible, what I was thinking was impossible. I opened the kitchen door and there she was. Clay dress, clay socks, clay shoes – but her body was flesh and blood. Phoebe was holding her.

Frank said, 'She's our daughter.'

These drugs – they bugger up my memory.

Chapter Thirty-Four

I'm a tooth hanging by a thread. One yank and I'll be gone. The doctors tell me that I've enough morphine in me to kill a cow. I must be a bull.

Joke, Mr Jones.

I signed the Official Secrets Act . . . swore I would never talk about this until the day I died. Well, it's night, it's not day, and I'm dying . . . But, Mr Jones, I broke my promise once before.

About a week later, Phoebe told me about Mari and the stone. Mari had said it had fallen from the sky . . . given one to her schoolfriend, Rex Muller, the brother of the boy who came back from the dead. That explained Lazarus . . .

People had seen those stones falling. The stones were a matter of great interest on the base. They'd searched for them but not found any. What they found was . . . was more valuable . . . They found the body of an alien being. Forgot the stones. Believed they weren't important. Wrong.

Phoebe and Frank let it be known that they'd adopted Skye. Peculiar little girl . . . silent, wordless, still. I did my damnedest to make sure no questions were asked.

When I went back to Bentwaters, I worked on data. It was a dull job . . . I think they were testing me. Must've passed the test because I was promoted . . . became one of the top technicians on the Doubleday project.

I never spoke to Frank about my work . . . he never asked . . .

Enough. Forgive me. I can't . . . what . . . ?

Ah, is this what I think it is? It feels so good just to hold . . . give me a moment . . .

Wow. I feel clear in my head for the first time since I've been in here.

Yes, I remember, Mr Jones.

It took two years. We used the alien body that was found in the forest and created the first half-alien, half-magnetic being. Scientists had found a way to create cyber skin, using nano-wires to mesh with alien cells, producing a synthetic skin that was part living, part electronic. The ultimate success would be if Doubleday could live within society undetected. He was to be monitored every step of the way.

Oh, Mr Jones, I can't tell you what it feels like to think straight.

Remember, this was years ago – what we were doing was beyond the conceived idea of what was possible. Then, disaster: almost immediately after he was released he went missing. Reports came in of a young punk who had stolen from shops in the Ipswich area. People who encountered him talked of his strength. They used words like 'not human' and 'alien'.

The Doubleday we had sent out was a respectable-looking young man in a suit, could have been a salesman. The picture of this punk did not correspond with any of our data.

By then I was living at the barracks on the airbase and hadn't been in touch with Phoebe and Frank for a while. Because of Skye, I'd thought it would be safer if I separated myself from them.

One day – about three weeks after Doubleday had gone missing – Phoebe phoned me in a terrible state. She said she was worried sick because Skye had started talking.

I said, 'That's good, isn't it?'

Phoebe said it wasn't the talking that was freaking her out but what Skye was saying.

I drove to Shingle Street that evening. When I arrived Skye was just staring out of the window. Phoebe told me that she kept saying the same thing, over and over. 'Doubleday is out there, he's looking for Icarus.'

I felt sick. Not that Icarus, surely? Not the Icarus who walked through a steel door?

I said, 'Who's Icarus?' hoping with all my heart that Phoebe would say she hadn't a clue.

Instead, she said, 'He's a friend. But I don't know who Doubleday is.'

Skye turned around and looked at me.

'Uncle Mark,' she said. 'You know who Icarus is. You kept him secret. Doubleday wants Icarus to make him whole again.'

I tell you, Mr Jones, she was the creepiest little girl I'd ever met. How she knew all that I had no idea. I asked her and she said nothing more.

Shortly after Phoebe had put Skye to bed, Frank came home.

'Do you know what she's talking about?' he asked me.

I said I did.

We sat in the kitchen and looked out of the French windows onto the dark beach and heard the sea hitting the shore. In the distance the container ships, lights twinkling, were parked on the horizon.

Over macaroni cheese I broke all the rules and told Frank and Phoebe about the stones that had dropped from the UFO, about the alien corpse that had been found in Rendlesham Forest, how Doubleday had been created out of the dead alien's organs. And how Icarus and Ishmael had disappeared in front of my eyes.

Phoebe said, 'Do you think Doubleday's after Skye's stone? It's the same as the one Lazarus had. Do you know about Lazarus?'

Oh yes, the Darkstar Programme knew about him all right. They were making sure his parents stayed suitably numb. You know the Pink Floyd song, Mr Jones? Maybe it isn't 'suitably'. I've forgotten . . . numb is right . . . 'Comfortably Numb', that's it.

I didn't think Doubleday was dangerous and said so. I didn't say that he had been programmed to find aliens.

But Phoebe said, 'Is Icarus an alien?'

One candle was alight on the kitchen table. There were no other lights and our reflections in the French windows shone back at us. Suddenly, Doubleday's face was staring in. We all froze. He looked anything but harmless. His eyes were red, his feet were bare. He fitted the description given in all the reports we'd had about the punk from Ipswich, reports no one had been able to follow up because Doubleday had disabled all his circuits so that no one had control over him. He'd pulled the synthetic skin from the back of his head. He looked like a monster, and I thought that's exactly what we had created. He stuck out his tongue, licked his lips and as he walked away from the house, the back of his head lit up.

My duty was to call the Darkstar Programme immediately, have him captured and taken back to the base. But I sat, not moving.

Frank said in a whisper, 'What are you going to do?'

I said, 'I have to shut him down before his handlers find him.'

'We are in deep trouble if he's found,' said Frank. 'Aren't we?'

I nodded. The Darkstar Programme wouldn't hesitate to do what was necessary to keep their latest toy top secret.

I came up with a plan of sorts. I said we would have to trap him, trick him into believing that Icarus was here.

It was Phoebe, I think, who came up with the idea of her mother's pantry. She said she was sure her mother would help us. She was very fond of Icarus.

There is a saying, Mr Jones. It has to do with a shitty creek, a leaking boat and a paddle. You've heard it. Well, that's where we were – up that creek.

Frank suggested the portrait that Phoebe had recently painted of Icarus might be enough to fool Doubleday, might lure him into Mrs Berry's pantry. I hadn't seen it and hoped he was right. I went to work, figuring out how to shut down Doubleday's energy source, how to make his world lightless.

Next morning, Phoebe went to London to pick up the

painting. She took Skye with her, even though Skye didn't want to go.

Mrs Berry was a remarkably brave and calm woman. When we told her our plan, she just said yes. She said Icarus – and Skye – must be protected. So we emptied the pantry, blocked up the window, made sure there wasn't a crack left for sunshine to sneak in. Then I placed Phoebe's portrait of Icarus on the back wall and hung a lamp above it. The portrait was incredibly realistic, one of the finest paintings she'd ever done. I put a pair of shoes on the floor. The effect was good enough. In the gloom, it looked like Icarus was standing there, waiting for Doubleday.

Phoebe wrote a note in case someone should find Doubleday and accidentally let him out.

Skye had the stone with her and around tea-time, she became very agitated, saying, 'He's here, he's here, Doubleday's here.' Phoebe and Mrs Berry went upstairs with Skye. I told Frank to go with them but he insisted on staying with me. He was my older brother, after all.

I opened the back door and we waited for Doubleday to walk in. The second he saw the painting in the pantry he went towards it, calling to Icarus. As I'd anticipated, his brain was so destroyed he couldn't tell what was real and what wasn't. The second he was inside we slammed the door shut and turned off the light. And I just hoped that I had sufficiently blocked his energy source and he wouldn't have enough power to break out.

He battered at the door for some time, shouting, 'You've tricked me, Icarus, you've tricked me. Again you've let me down. I will find you, Icarus, and I will have my revenge.'

After a while, the banging on the door became a tapping and his fury abated, his voice becoming weaker. It was dreadful to hear him.

'Icarus,' he said, 'don't do this, my comrade. Help me. Only you can help me – I need a stone. Icarus, it's me, I am Troyon, I am your kinsman . . . don't forsake me.'

On and on he went until the words petered out and at last, all was quiet. Frank and I spent the night in the kitchen. The following morning, we taped over the door and painted it, pushed the dresser in front of it, went back to work as if nothing had happened. I told myself that the Darkstar Programme had no idea what we'd done.

Two days later, Frank and Phoebe were killed in a car crash. I was told it was a police matter, investigation was under way. We never knew what caused their deaths. I had lost the people most dear to me and I was only still alive because Darkstar needed me. I felt close to breaking down. They wanted me on medication but I wouldn't take it.

One night, I was in a very bad way. I was stumbling back to the airbase; it was pitch black but in the beam of my torch I saw Icarus. Where he came from, I don't know. Just like the deer, he appeared from nowhere. I told him about the alien's corpse, what they'd done to it. I hoped he might kill me, then all the grief would be over. He was very quiet and then said, 'You were brave. You did the right thing.'

It was five years before I saw him again.

Phoebe's mother was amazing. She looked after her strange

granddaughter, protected her like a lioness until . . .

I went to see her after they'd jumped, after Icarus had been arrested. I wanted to say how sorry I was. Mrs Berry looked at me as if I was as thick as a bench. She said that they had to go home, they couldn't have stayed here. I said I didn't know why Icarus hadn't gone with them.

She sighed. Simple, Icarus came here to learn about love and that takes time and it meant learning about sorrow as well.

What time is it, Mr Jones?

Three? In the morning?

No, I don't want to sleep. I have all eternity for that pleasure.

After my brother died I wanted to leave the Darkstar Programme. But once you've signed on the line, you're there for life.

It was a relief when they sent me to America to retrain for undercover work. I returned to England and was given time off, told they would call on me when I was needed. Didn't have to wait long. Icarus was sent to prison, to be kept in solitary confinement. I became his prison officer. I never minded. It was a pleasure; he was an extraordinary man. We became very close. I miss him. I think of him as one of the best friends I have ever known. He had many opportunities to escape. He could walk through a wall as if it was tissue paper. He often did but he always came back. Darkstar instructed me to turn a blind eye. I asked Icarus why he didn't just leave. He said he wasn't ready but when he was, he would be gone. Eventually, they put him in an open prison. I was no longer needed. I fooled myself for a while that I was free of the Darkstar Programme. I liked the idea of being my own boss and started a chimney-sweeping business, bought a van, the works. But no one is ever free of those people.

I heard from an ex-colleague who still worked in the prison service that this girl, who had written a bestseller, had been given permission to visit Icarus. I didn't realise immediately that I'd met her, swept the chimney at her parents' house in Orford. A few days later, Icarus walked through the wall for the last time. He'd found what he'd been searching for. It was time for him to leave.

People said horrible things at the inquest, that Icarus had groomed her, that he was a paedophile. He wasn't. He was that rare being – genuine, honest, and when at last he found love, passionate. He loved Becky enough to let her go; she didn't have to return with him. But she wasn't going to leave him. She was too like him – out there, not of this world.

Have you seen Mari Scott, Mr Whoever-You-Are? She must've gone through hell. Still going through hell. I regret that I couldn't tell Mari Scott, or his girlfriend, what had happened to Alex. I couldn't, but I knew. After all, I was there. She was beautiful, his girlfriend. Her name was . . . the name of a plant . . . smells so sweet, smells of life. Summer blossom, perfumes hot nights . . . jasmine. Jazmin. Jaz for short. Both of them, Mari and Jazmin, deserve the truth. Now it's too late. The official story is that he went missing the day Becky and Icarus jumped. He did, but not in the way people thought.

Chapter Thirty-Five

I must have fallen asleep. Are you still here, Mr Jones? Good, glad you didn't leave. What's the time? You don't know, I don't know and you are right, it doesn't matter.

Well, I'm still here and my head doesn't feel scrambled so I can say I feel better, thank you for asking. Do you want this back?

Where was I? You see, Mr Jones, I was with Icarus for so long, I knew him, he knew me. Because I was working undercover it was difficult to form any other relationships, so we only had each other. We were both prisoners in a way and we became very close. When he told me he was going home and taking Becky, I knew he meant it. He needed access to a high building and asked if I would help him. I told him that the only way would be if I informed the bigwigs at Darkstar. I thought they would cooperate in order to catch a sighting of a UFO at close range. It was a risk but there was no way it could be done without them. I never said where Icarus was, or how I'd found him, but I suspected they knew. They knew everything. They let Icarus go home because they wanted Doubleday back. He'd been a

209

multi-million-dollar project that had walked into oblivion only to reappear to cause havoc. It was becoming harder to keep his trail of destruction invisible, especially after the violent murder of the minicab driver.

I persuaded them that Doubleday was likely to turn up if he knew that Icarus was going to try to leave. I didn't tell them that he was after a stone. But the fact that Becky was prepared to travel with Icarus intrigued them even more. She would be the first human to make such a journey. That fascinated the scientists at Darkstar. They had observed Skye and Lazarus, had watched them jump, but Skye and Lazarus, they had realised, weren't human.

The day I went to fetch Icarus and Becky, I told Alex and Jazmin that I would be back for them in the evening and that on no account were they to leave the flat or let anyone in.

It was getting dark when Icarus, Becky and me arrived at the Shard. It was unfinished but it was high enough for our purpose. Darkstar had made sure it had been evacuated on the pretence of a suspect package. The whole area had been cordoned off. Police everywhere.

It was eerily quiet as we made our way up in the lift, the only sound the wind whistling through the unfinished walls.

Everything went according to plan. We were waiting on the highest platform. There must have been about thirty of us, though it was quite hard to see. Icarus had given us the time his craft was expected. At ten o'clock the countdown began. It was a perfect cloudy night. London lay below us – patches of jewelled light. Then Control at Darkstar spotted the craft on the radar. I was listening through my earpiece to the countdown . . . ten, nine, eight, seven . . . when I received the message. Doubleday was on his way up. He had a hostage with him. Six, five, four . . . We braced ourselves as Doubleday came out of the lift, dragging with him a body. It was Alex. Doubleday was holding him by the arm, as if he was a puppet. Alex appeared to be unconscious, his face bloodied. Doubleday dropped him on the platform.

The second Doubleday saw Icarus, he shouted at him. 'How could you have abandoned me? You left me, Icarus, you left me. I will kill you for that.'

He ran towards Icarus and stopped. Everything stopped. A shadow fell on the platform and then it was there: a huge, silver, triangular-shaped cloud silently hovering over us, its lights blue and red. It lined up just below the platform. I don't remember how they appeared but, one by one, on the edge of the platform stood a line of the most extraordinarily beautiful beings I have ever seen. Like Icarus and Ishmael, they looked just as you would imagine humans who never age or outgrow their time might, humans whose bodies aren't broken by gravity. By comparison we looked like uniformed insects, corrupted by the lives we live and the lies we tell.

Becky turned, perhaps to take a last look at us, I don't know. It was then she saw Alex. Icarus held her back as one of their number stepped forward. He wore a top hat and dark glasses but I knew I had seen him before . . .

Everyone from Darkstar was paralysed, we could do nothing. Even Doubleday was losing his power.

'A stone,' he said, his voice slurred and faltering. 'I want a stone, a stone, a stone.'

The alien in the top hat put his hand out and with one gesture lifted Doubleday and held him suspended about three metres above us.

The alien said to us, 'Your people have made too many monsters. Too many monsters have made too much misery for this world. You do not need another one.'

He left Doubleday suspended and gently picked up Alex. Followed by his people, he carried him onto the craft, leaving Becky and Icarus by themselves.

They stood on the edge of the building, the craft hovering below them, and Icarus took Becky's hand.

I heard him say, 'Jump, Becky, jump.'

If she hesitated, I didn't see it.

Then they were gone.

Doubleday fell down onto the platform, a collection of broken parts.

They say a sonic boom was heard over London that night. Computers crashed, trains stopped, planes failed to take off. Those that were in mid-flight hung in the air, not moving. For half an hour we were shown what would happen if all the plugs were pulled on our electronic lives.

I don't know if Alex survived what Doubleday did to him. I can't tell you that.

I was granted my freedom from the Darkstar Programme as long as I was prepared to be the scapegoat in court. At the time it seemed a small price to pay. Now I know it cost me everything.

Mr Jones, I'm pleased I've said all those words. Thank you for coming – and thank you for this.

And, Mr Jones, I know who you are.

MATRON OF ST MARY'S HOSPICE, CUMBRIA

Chapter Thirty-Six

Mr Jones, I cannot thank you enough for staying with him. He looks very peaceful. What's that he is holding? Most strange. I'm not exactly sure it's . . . You have a point, Mr Jones. If it brings him comfort, what harm can it do?

Yes, certainly. I'll give it to him when he wakes up – if he does wake up. Let me see if I can read your writing . . . 'Live your life, find love. Start again.'

Is that correct?

JAZMIN LITTLE

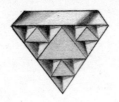

Chapter Thirty-Seven

Don't make me do this, Mr Jones, don't make me remember any more. Especially not the night Becky jumped. Isn't it better not to remember?

You're right, how can I ever forget? Perhaps it would have been better if I had never met Alex, never loved him. Then at least I could have tried to live again. That is the night I died too, you know. My heart may still be ticking but that's about the sum total of it.

All right, I will try to reach the end of my story . . .

The flat had an eerie sound to it after Icarus and Becky left. Not just the everyday sounds – distant conversation, pipes gurgling, toilets being flushed. No, this was static, crackling, as if a radio wasn't tuned in right and was trying to find a station. We didn't have a radio.

'Listen,' I said. 'What is that?'

Alex said, 'I don't know. Weird.' He went to the side of the window and carefully looked out. In the street light there was nobody there. 'Why does it all feel so wrong, so . . . electric?'

Alex went into the kitchen to put the kettle on. Water

bubbling away is a comforting noise. I told myself to stop thinking about the static – most probably it was coming from another flat. The walls weren't that thick. I followed Alex into the kitchen.

'You know all those alien books that Becky has?' I said, desperate to think about something else. 'Did you ever read any of them?'

'Yep. Some. Why?'

'I have, and not one of those stories about alien invasions ever talks about a snake-free Garden of Eden planet. Usually in those books, the aliens want humans for their organs, not their emotions.'

Alex smiled. 'You think Icarus should have brought a brochure with him, advertising the good life to be lived on the edge of our solar system?'

'Might have helped. You're making fun of me.'

'No. Just thinking that I love you.'

I put my arms around his neck. 'Do you really, really mean it?'

He took his silver ring – his lucky ring – off his little finger. He looked so serious. He slipped it on my wedding-ring finger.

'Well, that's done it,' I said. 'Though I think we're a bit young.'

He laughed. It was good to hear him laugh. It was good to laugh. It didn't last long.

The kettle was just about to boil when there was a loud bang and the power went off.

'I don't like this,' I said. 'I don't like this one little bit.'

Just then all the lights in the flat started flashing. The television switched itself on and Becky's laptop rebooted itself.

We ran into the narrow hall and froze. The wooden front door with a steel panel on the outside had become nothing more than a membrane, thin enough that an outline of a face could be seen peering through. Doubleday materialised, his red eyes wild. Everything in the flat crackled with his power.

It paralysed us. He forced himself against the membrane until it became liquid and he lurched through it into the flat. He pushed me out of the way and took hold of Alex.

'Any trouble, I will kill her,' he said to him.

Alex tried to punch him in the stomach. He shouldn't have done that.

Doubleday threw him across the room, picked him up and threw him again. There was nothing I could do. I screamed for help but no sound came. Alex was unconscious. Doubleday came to me and put his finger hard on my forehead so that my head began to ache. Then he was gone, and so was Alex.

I tried to open the front door and follow them but I couldn't. Everything I did felt like it was in slow motion. I managed to get to the window. Outside the main entrance I could see a van with blacked-out windows. Doubleday threw Alex in and the doors shut.

That was the last time I ever saw Alex. I couldn't save him. I couldn't do anything, not even call for help. I couldn't keep my eyes open. The feeling of leaden exhaustion overwhelmed me. I was battling to stay awake, to move my limbs.

I woke up in the Royal Free Hospital. The police questioned me a lot about Alex and all I could tell them was that the last time I'd seen him was when he'd been kidnapped by Doubleday.

I was accused of taking drugs and of encouraging my best friend to commit suicide. They said I was making it all up about the two creeps, about Doubleday. For a long time I really thought Icarus and Becky had jumped to their deaths. I was finally told no bodies had been found at the foot of the Shard.

Please, Mr Jones, answer one bloody question: what is the point of remembering any of this shit?

Chapter Thirty-Eight

After Mr Jones left, I wrote a long letter to Mari. I didn't write with my usual, tentative, 'I'm sorry' approach but with the confidence that Mr Jones had given me. If nothing else, this was my story, my side of the diamond, once cloudy, now bright. Taking Becky's notebook in the playground that day changed everything for me, and I know it did the same for her.

When such momentous events happen, ones that affect the lives of so many people, each person must be allowed to tell their truth. What makes the diamond shine bright is the way it's cut. I had the right to my side of the story and I wrote it without regret. The same in my letters to Ruth and Simon but I kept theirs brief. And finally I dropped a line to my Auntie Karen. I didn't bother with Mum. She'd washed her hands of me long ago.

I've always been tidy. I didn't want to leave the bedsit in a mess so I hoovered and cleaned it all, then had a bath and put the towels in the washing machine. I ate what was left in the fridge and propped up a note on the table, explaining what I was about to do. I closed the front door and put the keys under the mat. I took the rubbish out with me and posted the four letters. I didn't want the police losing letters again.

I decided I would walk to Blackfriars. It's not far from Dalston. It was one of those beautiful evenings when London can break your heart.

The William Shakespeare – or WS – Tower had been completed three months earlier. It was built to straddle the entrance to the new London Bridge, which had houses and shops on it. The WS Tower rose higher than the Shard. It was an extraordinary piece of architecture, combining wood and steel with glass. 'A village in the sky' was how it was described. At the very top there was to be a garden. I had watched the tower being built and as soon as it opened, I managed to get a job there as a cleaner.

That evening, I clocked in as usual. I liked working nights. There was hardly anyone about and the guards knew me, no one questioned me. The entrance hall is truly breathtaking. When you walk in you look up at a cathedral ceiling made of wood. I waited for the first of the three lifts. My pass only took me as far as the second lift; after that I would have to hope I could manage the third lift without being detected. I knew that was the only tricky part of my plan.

When I arrived at the third lift, the doors were open as if waiting for me.

I looked around. I could see no one so I quickly pressed the button to the top. Perhaps then I should have realised that this wasn't quite right. I mean, no one had been up to the roof garden apart from those who worked on it. The grand opening was to be the following week.

I was feeling very calm, incredibly peaceful. I didn't really give much thought as to why it had all been so easy when it shouldn't have been. I was concentrating on what I would do when I got up there.

When people talk of roof gardens, you think, yeah, a couple of trees in pots, lots of wooden decking and a few dismal-looking plants scattered around.

But this was astonishing. There was an orchard, a small lake – so beautiful – and all around was the City of London. I walked through an arbour to the far side of the garden. My plan was simple, neat. I would keep on walking and be buried and forgotten in the silt of the Thames.

The sunset made everything golden. I felt no fear, just relief that at last it was all over.

He was sitting on a folding chair beside a folding table laid with a paper cloth, a bottle of champagne and two glasses.

'What are you doing here, Mr Jones? What is this?'

'It's a scene from a brochure. You said to Alex it would help if there was a brochure. I thought you might like to have a glass of champagne and, if you still wished to jump into the river after all I have to tell you, I wouldn't stop you.'

I was so wrong-footed that I sat down.

'How did you know I was coming here?'

'You told me when you said you were going away. You've told me from the very beginning that you knew the end, your end. And here you are.' He popped the cork. 'You see, I have learned a lot from you about what love is,' he said. 'I came to this planet with the naive belief that it would be simple to introduce to our people an emotion that you humans take for granted. What I have learned is that love in all its various guises – maternal love, fraternal love, the love of friends – is far more complicated. True love is a power, perhaps the most powerful thing that the human species possesses. It creates music, art, poetry, but more than that, it can survive through space and time. A strawberry? They came with the champagne.'

I took one.

'Who are you?' I asked.

'My name is Ishmael. Among my people I am considered a wise man. However, I showed little understanding, let alone wisdom, when I imagined that an emotion as complex as love would be easy to take back to our race. When Icarus led me from imprisonment on the airbase, I told him he was to stay here and return only if he found love and knew it for what it was. Lazarus and Skye were the first to come but Skye was made from clay and Lazarus from a dead boy's skin, both only given life by our stones. Their emotion was not so much love for each other as a desire to be where they belonged. When Icarus returned with Becky and Alex there was much rejoicing until it became clear that Alex's unhappiness stemmed from being separated from you. It had never occurred to us that with love came longing.

'I returned to Earth to discover for myself the nature of what we have taken on. When I met Mari, her heartbreak over her son moved me, showed me love doesn't die, even when the one who is loved is absent. But it is you, Jazmin, who taught me the true power of the emotion. At first, you greatly puzzled me, for your future appeared tied to the past by the loss of love. I found you felt the same as Alex, to such an extent that you would prefer to take your life rather than live without him.'

'Are you telling me Alex is alive?'

'Yes. I cannot show you the brochure but you have my word.'

'He's waiting for me?'

'Yes. I've been again to see Mari, to tell her what has happened to her son. I've told her where Alex is and that he is well, that he loves her and always will. I don't know if she believed me. Do you believe me?'

'Wait – say that again – Alex is alive?'

'I could have brought proof – pictures – but I have been told that this emotion we seek is blind and one must learn to fall into the unknown in order to find love waiting there.'

Mr Jones drained his glass. 'Shall we go?'

He took off his sunglasses. His eyes were dark like Icarus's.

'May I?' he said, and, taking my hand, he helped me onto the ledge.

Below was the Thames, London, the city so small it looked unreal. We waited. Then it was there – a triangular spacecraft hovering a metre below us.

For the first time, Mr Jones smiled at me.

'Come,' he said. 'Jump, Jazmin, jump.'

Author Note

I had been staying in Suffolk in a place called Shingle Street, where a friend of mine has a house. One day we went on a walk to Rendlesham Forest. I wanted to see where the supposed UFO landing had taken place. We became incredibly lost and managed not to follow the trail but to walk in a different direction and both of us got very spooked out. I had with me my little dog Lottie, a dachshund with very small legs. By the time we had walked in circles for about two hours, the sun was setting. We managed to find a road, and a Land Rover stopped to give us a lift. In it was an American family. They asked us where we had been and what we were doing. I said I was very interested in the Rendlesham Forest UFO incident. Whereupon the grandmother said, 'I was there and what I saw that day I will never talk about, never. Those that did got into a lot of trouble.'

I asked, 'Do you believe it was real?'

She replied, 'As I said, I will not talk about those strange things.'

Stories come to you and just sit on your shoulder and if you're lucky enough they begin to whisper in your ear. Shortly after this incident I got into a taxi going to Woodbridge and the driver said, 'You'll never guess who I had in my cab.' He mentioned the American who had been in charge of the airbase at Woodbridge when the UFO incident happened in 1980. What he had seen that day ruined his career and he was brave enough to speak out about it. He had come back to give a lecture about Rendlesham. The taxi driver had asked him if he believed it had happened, to which the gentleman said, 'I know it. I saw it.'

My Side of the Diamond is a story about love. The question really is, what makes us human? I wondered what would happen if you had an alien planet where the inhabitants were perfectly kind and respectable to one another, had no desire to kill or to love, believed in no god in particular. They brought up their children well, with respect, but they had no love for them. That got me thinking about what the essence of love is, not just the love between two people or the love of family. Out of love springs great creativity that has given us music, words, paintings. You could argue that it is the cornerstone of all creativity.

So how would you take love back to your planet? What are the risks involved in doing so?

Discussion Notes

- Jazmin and Becky meet at the same secondary school and although they come from the same area, their backgrounds are quite different. What do you think brought the two girls together as friends and what do you think they value in each other's friendship?

- The story is told through different characters talking to a mysterious 'Mr Jones'. None of the characters are quite sure what Mr Jones is researching for. What do you think Mr Jones was going to do with the information?

- Why do you think Sally Gardner used the phrase 'My Side of the Diamond' for the title?

- Icarus told Mari he had come to Earth to understand and find love. Do you think he succeeded? And if so, when?

- If you were Becky and had fallen in love with Icarus, would you jump with him?

Creative Writing Ideas

- Retell a story you know well, perhaps a fairy story, by pretending to be Mr Jones interviewing five of the characters of the story. How would each character tell their side of the 'diamond'?

- We hear the story of Becky's relationship with Icarus through Jazmin. How do you think Becky would tell the story? Write a passage in Becky's voice describing the group's night at the pub when they were joined by Icarus.

- When Doubleday broke into the Burnses' house Becky, Jaz and Alex had no memory of anything from the sound of someone coming up the stairs to two days later. Police thought they had taken drugs and trashed the house themselves. What do you think happened? Write a short extra chapter to explain what happened. Whose perspective will you tell the story from?

- Imagine you are helping Icarus to understand what love is. Using examples from the book, write a list of ways people might feel when they are in love.

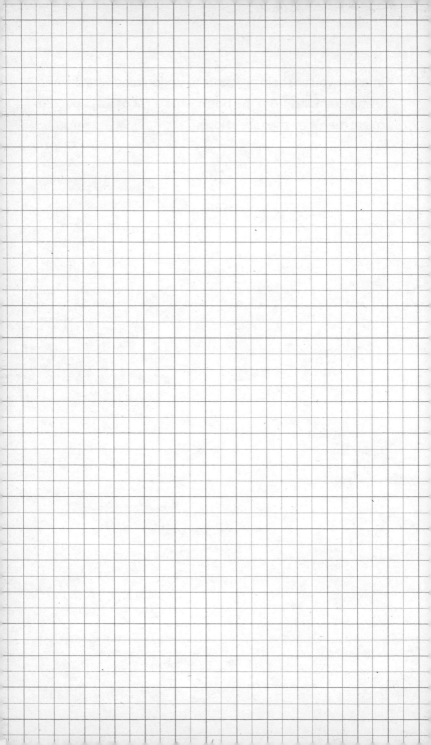

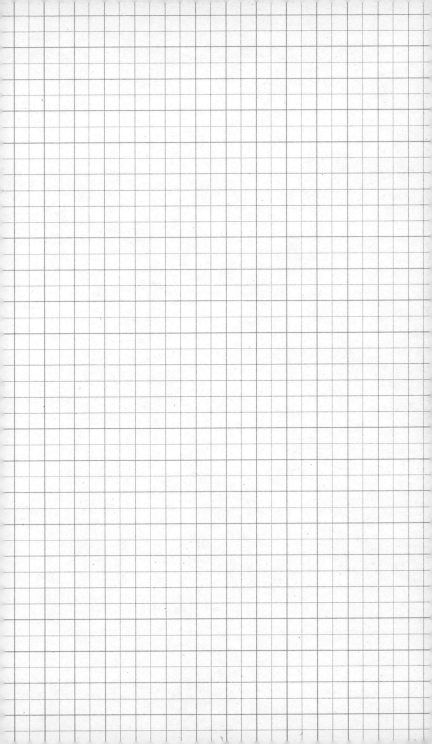

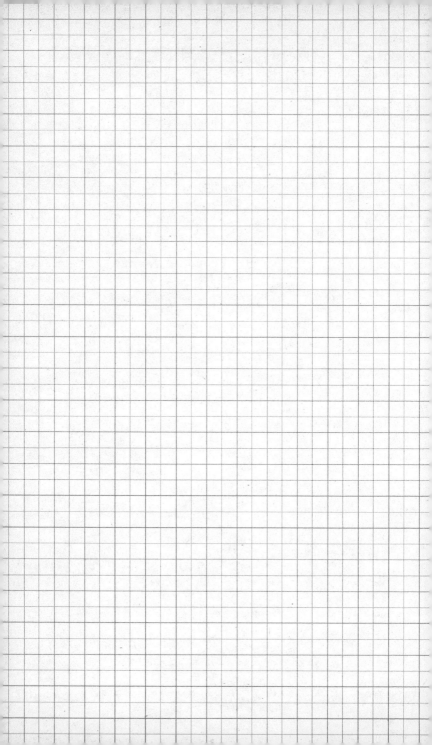

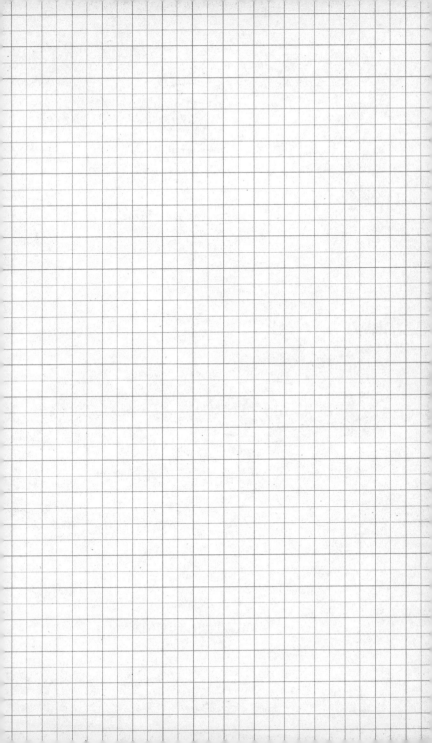

Sally Gardner

Sally Gardner is a multi-award-winning novelist whose work has been translated into more than twenty-two languages. Her novel *Maggot Moon* (Hot Key Books) won both the Costa Children's Book Prize and the Carnegie Medal 2013. Sally's genre-defying novel *The Double Shadow* (Orion) received great critical acclaim and was also longlisted for the Carnegie Medal 2013. *The Red Necklace* (shortlisted for 2007 *Guardian* Book Prize) and *The Silver Blade* are set during the French Revolution, and the film rights have been purchased by Dominic West. Sally also won the 2005 Nestlé Children's Book Prize for her debut novel *I, Coriander*. She is also author of the popular *Wings & Co* Fairy Detective Agency Series and *Tinder*, illustrated by David Roberts (Orion). Most recently she has published a novel for adults, *An Almond for a Parrot*. Follow Sally at www.sallygardner.net or on Twitter: @TheSallyGardner

Thank you for choosing a Hot Key book.

If you want to know more about our authors
and what we publish, you can find us online.

You can start at our website

www.hotkeybooks.com

And you can also find us on:

We hope to see you soon!